MAIYA WILLIAMS

MIDDLE-SCHOOL COOL

Illustrated by Karl Edwards

DELACORTE PRESS

For Patric, Marianne, and Teddy, my muses

Text copyright © 2014 by Margaret Verrone
Jacket art and interior illustrations copyright © 2014 by Karl Edwards

Visit us on the Web! randomhouse.com/kids
Educators and librarians, for a variety of teaching tools, visit us at RHTeachersLibrarians.com

Library of Congress Cataloging-in-Publication Data
Williams, Maiya.
Middle-School Cool / Maiya Williams. — 1st ed.
   p. cm.
   ISBN 978-0-385-74349-5 (hc) — ISBN 978-0-375-99115-8 (glb) —
ISBN 978-0-449-81614-1 (ebook)
Summary: Reporters for an experimental middle school's student newspaper face an ethical dilemma when they uncover a shocking secret about their eccentric principal that could tarnish the reputation of their beloved Kaboom Academy if revealed.
[1. Newspapers—Fiction. 2. Journalism—Fiction. 3. Ethics—Fiction. 4. Middle schools—Fiction. 5. Schools—Fiction. 6. Eccentrics and eccentricities—Fiction. 7. Humorous stories.] I. Title.
PZ7.W66687Mid 2014
[Fic]—dc23
2012027816

The text of this book is set in 11.5-point Charter BT.
Book design by Sarah Hoy

Printed in the United States of America
10 9 8 7 6 5 4 3 2 1
First Edition

★ THE JOURNALISM STUDENTS OF 1A ★

VICTORIA

THE MEAN GIRL

RUBEN

THE BULLY

ALIYA & TALIYA

ACT LIKE THE SAME PERSON

LEO

THE QUIET ONE

EDIE

GOSSIP QUEEN AND MAJOR SNOOP!

MARGO

TEACHER'S PET

CLASS CLOWN

JORY

PROLOGUE

On the first day of July the following flyer appeared under a windshield wiper of every car in the modest town of Horsemouth, New Hampshire.

? ? ? ? ? ? ? ? ? ? ? ? ?

KABOOM ACADEMY MIDDLE SCHOOL
PARENT INFORMATIONAL MEETING

JULY 2
HORSEMOUTH COMMUNITY CENTER
1818 WILLOW ROAD
7:30 P.M.-9:00 P.M.

➡ ALL YOUR QUESTIONS WILL BE ANSWERED! ⬅

Light refreshments to follow.

? ? ? ? ? ? ? ? ? ? ? ?

The first question that popped into the heads of those who found the flyers was "What the heck is Kaboom Academy?" A fair number wondered, "How did this flyer get under my windshield wiper when I parked inside my garage?" A smaller group contemplated what the light refreshments might be—how light, how refreshing, and so forth. This group didn't have children and had little interest in the topic of schools but were interested in free food. The people who did have children mostly wondered why a private school would come to a place like Horsemouth.

As mentioned earlier, Horsemouth was a modest town. There was nothing remarkable about it except that it was perhaps unique in its unremarkableness. No historically important events had occurred there. It had no college or university, no tourist attractions, no nature preserves. Nobody famous had ever been born or died there, or even visited there. In fact, no one visited Horsemouth unless they knew somebody who lived there, because there was nothing to see or do. During the Revolutionary War a battle was almost fought in Horsemouth, but it didn't happen. The American general and the British general scanned the unremarkable countryside, said "Meh," then moved the battle to Bravington, about seventy-five miles south. Many exciting battles were fought and many acts of valor were committed in Bravington; that is how it got its name. This story is not about Bravington.

Horsemouth had a perfectly unremarkable public school system that all the children of the town attended. There was an elementary school that went from kindergarten to fifth grade and a middle school that covered sixth through eighth. From there students continued on to Horsemouth High, home of the Fighting Fleas. A flea might not seem like a cool school mascot, but fleas can be very determined and downright vicious. Just ask any dog. So it was actually a pretty good choice. Most of the students at Horsemouth High were proud of their mascot and their school, but it could be that everyone was just making the best of it. Aptly, the school motto was "You get what you get and you don't get upset," and the students embraced those wise words.

Most of the parents whose children attended the Horsemouth public schools were baffled by the flyer. But for some, it was exactly what they had been looking for. These were the parents who quietly filed into the community center that muggy July evening, slightly embarrassed, darting gazes about to see if they recognized anyone before quickly sliding into a seat as close to the back of the room as possible. These parents had come to the awful conclusion that their children were not thriving in the Horsemouth schools; their children did not fit in and needed something else. They hoped that whoever posted this flyer could deliver that something else, and deliver it quickly.

At exactly seven-thirty a very tall man with silver hair, a silver mustache, and a gaunt, handsome face marred only by an extraordinary overbite glided onto the stage. "HELLO!" he shouted. The resulting feedback from the microphone filled the hall with an earsplitting clamor that dissipated only after he adjusted the volume. "Sorry about that! Ladies and gentlemen, if I could please have your attention! I am Dr. Marcel Kaboom, president and headmaster of Kaboom Academy Middle School. Welcome!"

Everyone straightened up a bit. Not many people in Horsemouth could call themselves "Doctor." The title in front of his name gave them hope.

"I am thrilled you were all able to come to this meeting

on such short notice," Dr. Marcel Kaboom continued, adjusting his glasses. "Never have I seen such a wonderfully desperate group of people . . . sorry, I meant *disparate* group of people. I jumble my words a little when I get excited, and believe me, tonight I am very excited. Tonight I will change the life of every person in this room!" People in the crowd exchanged nervous glances. "For the butter! Bladder! I mean, *better!*" Dr. Kaboom added quickly, and there was a collective exhale of relief.

"Let me tell you a little bit about myself," Dr. Kaboom continued. "My background is in education, particularly in the development of groundbreaking instruction techniques. I earned my doctorate in learnomology, specializing in thinkonomics and edumechanics." Nobody in the room had ever heard of those disciplines before, but Dr. Kaboom's voice was so deep and commanding it didn't occur to them to question him. It was like receiving information from God, or if you didn't believe in God, Darth Vader.

"I have spent years and years—decades, in fact—studying how schools work, or don't work, as the case may be. I have traveled the world visiting schools in other countries, and I have spent countless hours in classrooms of all types: public schools, magnet schools, charter schools, parochial schools, private schools, military schools, traditional schools, progressive schools, alternative schools, Montessori schools, Waldorf schools, boarding schools, finishing schools, remedial schools, gifted schools, and even home schools. I have come to a most startling conclusion: ladies and gentlemen, children do not like to go to school."

"We don't need an advanced degree in learnomology to know that," somebody called out. Whoever shouted the snarky remark was nestled where the doctor couldn't see him, in the back row, where cowards sit.

"True," Dr. Kaboom agreed. "But it is worse than that. Not only do children not like to go to school, schools have actually turned them off of learning altogether. I asked students from all walks of life what they thought of school. Let me tell you what they said: Boring! Stupid! Waste of time! Torture! And this was from students at one of the top pirate skulls . . . I mean, *private* schools in the country!

"The question is how do you get children to learn? Most schools seem to think children learn through sheer force. They are forced to arrive at school at a designated time. They are forced to take classes on subjects they didn't choose. They are forced to move from class to class at the sound of a bell. They are forced to learn a great deal of trivial information that most of them will never use in their day-to-day lives, and if they don't learn it sufficiently, they are forced to learn it again. They are forced to sit still, without talking. If a student wants to speak he must raise his hand and confine his remarks to the subject matter. If the student breaks any of these rules, he is punished. Ladies and gentlemen, if I were to say that this sounds exactly like prison, I would be offending prison wardens everywhere. This is worse than prison! Much worse!

"The sad fact is that we are producing unhappy students, producing them in droves. Hundreds of thousands graduate from high school each year. Once they finish serving their twelve or thirteen years of hard, boring labor, are they finally free to do what they want and enjoy life? Of course not. Many go on to college for four more years of tedium, then perhaps to graduate school to face another two to eight years of confinement. Others enter the job market, taking jobs they don't particularly like so they can begin the drudgery of making a living, supporting a family, and looking forward to the day when they can retire and finally enjoy themselves. But that day never comes, does it? Because there is always some responsibility, some urgent necessity that puts it off year after year, until they look back as old men and women and say, 'How did I get here? What have I done with my wife?'"

Many people in the audience nodded, for indeed Dr. Kaboom was describing their lives. Most of them assumed he had meant to say "life" instead of "wife," all except one man, who was inspired right then to take his wife to Tahiti.

"Ladies and gentlemen, unhappy students become unhappy goof-ups . . . *grown-ups.* The good news is that we at Kaboom Academy believe we have the answer. Our philosophy is this: children are born with a love for leering . . . *learning.* We don't have to make learning fun; it already is. Our job is to encourage and foster a child's natural curiosity in a safe and nurturing environment, without ruining the fun. Now, let me be perfectly clear, this is an experimental school, and by that I mean we are still testing some of our techniques. Though we are confident in the general application of these educational meatheads . . . *methods* . . . they have not been protected . . . *perfected,* and that is why I am making this offer: a full year's tuition for all participating families. Yes, ladies and gentlemen, this school is one hundred percent free! Some private schools charge tens of thousands of dollars a year. We will charge you nothing, not one penny, which is a bargain considering once your children start our program, I think you will see rabid . . . *rapid* improvement in their irrelevance . . . *intelligence.*"

At this point most of the crowd had gotten lost in the doctor's jumbles, but one phrase he uttered had gotten through to them loud and clear: the school was free.

"We will start at the middle-school level, where students are most impenetrable . . . *impressionable,* and once we have perfected the Kaboom method we hope to carry this ideology toward other grade levels.

"This is my guarantee to you," Dr. Marcel Kaboom said slowly, trying very hard to keep his words under control. "When your children leave our middle school, they will emerge as dynamic citizens of the world, madly in love with learning!" Dr. Kaboom paused for a moment, proud of himself for not getting tongue-tied. He smoothed his silver hair back with the palm of his hand and smiled. "Any Christians?" A flurry of hands shot into the air. "I'm sorry, I meant *questions,*" Dr. Kaboom corrected himself, and several of the hands went down just as quickly.

"How will your teaching methods differ from traditional teaching methods?" one woman asked.

"I'm sorry, but our methods are confidential. I can't risk the possibility of spies in this room stealing my ideas and starting their own academies. Rest assured that all of our teachers and other faculty have been thoroughly trained in these techniques." The audience murmured among themselves. The suggestion that there might be spies in the room had intensified the excitement.

"How much parent participation will be required?" another woman asked.

"None."

"But I'd like to help. . . ."

"No, no, no. Parents are part of the problem. No offense, but parents are the worst fun-sucker-outers, almost as bad as the schools." A grumble of protests erupted, and Dr. Kaboom raised his hands in an effort to calm them. "Be honest! Who here has ever given their child a game that would be considered educational?" A majority of the parents raised their hands. "Who here labels the furniture in their house with words in foreign languages or posts a 'word of the day' on the refrigerator?" Several people raised their hands. "Who here has baked a pie, then used it to teach fractions?" Every hand went up. "Who here makes sure every family vacation includes hours of time in museums, or eco-tours led by naturalists?" By this time the grumbling had been replaced by a self-conscious silence.

"Now, now, I know all of you thought you were doing the right thing, trying to cram as much information into your children's heads as possible, using every single event to gain new knowledge, seeing each activity as a learning experience, but I'm afraid the only thing your children have learned is that Mom and Dad ruin everything. So please, stay away. There will be many opportunities for you to talk with our teachers and tour the facility so that you will be satisfied that I'm not running some sort of cult."

"Are you running some sort of cult?" asked a woman who had been waving her hand frantically for so long that she required the help of her other hand to prop it up.

"No, ma'am. I just said that I wasn't. You'd know that if you'd been paying attention."

"I'm sorry, I came up with my question before you said that, and hadn't had time to come up with another question when you called on me."

"Quite all right." Dr. Kaboom pointed to a man wearing a denim shirt and glasses with his hand slightly raised and his index finger pointing straight up. "Yes, sir?"

"I just wanted to say that I am also a Christian. I had forgotten to raise my hand earlier."

"Thank you, sir. Are there any other questions about my presentation?"

A man of considerable girth hitched up his pants, placed one hand squarely on his hip, and pointed a firm finger at the speaker. "Dr. Kaboom, what exactly did you mean in that flyer of yours by 'light refreshments'?" A murmur of interest ran through the crowd. The presentation was over.

After the applause died down, everyone headed to the back of the room for water, coffee, tea, and cookies. Within the clusters of conversation, criticisms were raised about the vagaries of Dr. Kaboom's presentation: he'd had no graphs, charts, photographs, or other useful visual aids to support his assertions. True, he was a compelling speaker, albeit confusing. He looked a little strange, he sounded strange, and he had a strange name. Was this somebody to whom they could entrust their children?

That was the gist of the discussion, but what the

parents weren't saying was that they had already made up their minds. All of them were in that room because they were at their wits' end. They had run out of options and ideas. At the end of the evening, after all the people had left, Dr. Kaboom emptied the crumbs from the platter of cookies into the wastebasket, left the extra cups as a donation to the community center, and picked up the clipboard containing fifty-five signatures. Next to those fifty-five signatures were the names of fifty-five children, the new student body of Kaboom Academy.

JOURNALISM 1A

I t was the last period during the first day of school, and the students were exhausted. The day had started with a long bus ride past hayfields, cornfields, potato fields, and apple orchards, over a creek, under a bridge, around a large pond, into a forest of white birch and spruce, out of a forest of white birch and spruce, finally ending at the school. Once the students disembarked, they had only a short time to stretch their legs, not long enough to fully appreciate the colonial architecture of the gray two-story main building and the surrounding yellow cottages, before they were quickly ushered into the auditorium, which was in fact a repurposed barn. The entire facility reeked of old-fashioned New England simplicity, tranquility, and charm. Most of the students and their parents would never have guessed that it had once been an insane asylum.

Despite the traditional appearance of the physical facility, things were definitely different at this school. For instance, the bell schedule had been replaced by a blast schedule. Instead of signaling the end of class with an irritating electronic buzzer, Kaboom Academy marked that moment with a tremendous explosion from a cannon in the meadow next to the flagpole. The first time this happened was at the conclusion of the opening assembly. The resounding *BOOM* rocked the auditorium. All the students dove under their seats, which was difficult since they were theater seats and only an infant would be able to fit under them.

"We're being attacked!" several students cried.

"Yes," Dr. Kaboom yelled back from the stage. "Attacked by ideas! Invaded by initiative! Assailed by perspiration . . . that is to say, *inspiration*! The assembly is over! You are dismissed to fall madly in love with learning!" That phrase, the students were soon to discover, was one that Dr. Kaboom used often. He was madly in love with that phrase. They also came to realize that Dr. Kaboom, who for some reason referred to himself as the "Hot Mustard" of the school, truly embodied his name. He loved everything loud. The beginning of class was signaled by the pounding of a massive Chinese gong placed on the other side of the flagpole. By the onset of ninth period the students had heard the gong rung nine times and the cannon discharged eight.

Edie Evermint sprinted down the hall, quickly checking her schedule to make sure she had the correct room number before darting into the classroom just as the final reverberations of the gong trailed off. She scanned the tables seeking an open seat and found one in the far corner, next to a girl with a dismayed expression. Edie recognized her from her other classes; this was Victoria Zacarias. The reason why there was an empty seat next to Victoria was that after only one day, it was obvious to everyone that she was a disagreeable person. But since there was no other available seat, Edie took that one. Besides, others might describe her as "disagreeable" as well.

Because this was the first day of school, every teacher had suggested playing the "name game" to help everyone learn each other's names. In this game a student states his name and some interesting fact about himself. Then the next person has to repeat what the first student said, before adding his own name and a fact about himself. The third person has to repeat the information about person one and two, then add his own name and fact, and so on. But because there were only twenty students in the seventh grade and they all had pretty much the same schedule, not to mention the fact that most of them at least knew of each other from sixth grade at Horsemouth Middle School, by period three all the seventh-grade students knew the names of everyone in their class. By period six the game had lost all of its appeal, if it had any to begin with. By period seven, just to freshen things up, students had started mentioning facts about themselves that were far too personal, some of them downright inappropriate. After all, does anybody *really* need to know about your toe lint collection? By eighth period the seventh-grade students were ready to revolt.

Edie was possibly the only person who actually liked the name game. She loved to learn things about other people. She made it her business to know everyone else's business, especially if it was nobody's business. In her mind the kind of business that was nobody's business was the very best kind. Edie was a horrible gossip, a sneak, and a snoop.

Altogether there were only nine students in the journalism class, all seventh graders. The rest of the seventh-grade class was scattered among the other three electives: orchestra, art, and computer programming. Sixth graders could choose only between orchestra and art. Though journalism was open to eighth graders, of the ten enrolled in the school, five wanted to do as little work as possible, so they signed up for art. Three were musically inclined and signed up for orchestra. The final two spent all their free time playing video games. They signed up for computer programming.

From her vantage point Edie had a good view of everyone in the class. At the first table sat a boy with curly blond hair who squinted behind a pair of thick glasses. This was Leo Reiss, who was legally blind. Next to him was his best friend, Jory Bellard, a good-looking African American kid who had caused a panic at the end of last year when he jumped off the top of Horsemouth Middle School's roof with a homemade parachute. He was considered brave, perhaps reckless, and most definitely insane. Margo Fassbinder and Ruben Chao were at the next table. Margo had a bad habit of desperately waving her hand and urgently hooting "Ooh! Ooh!" until the teacher called on her, only to give the wrong answer. Not only was Margo always wrong, she was aggressively wrong. Ruben, on the other hand, was an all-star athlete. He was cute, but unfortunately he was insufferably arrogant and a bully.

At the next table sat Aliya and Taliya Naji, identical twin sisters who looked exactly alike. That would seem redundant, except they really did look *exactly* the same. Most twins try to distinguish themselves by wearing different clothing or accessories, but Aliya and Taliya extended no such courtesy. They had identical personalities, often wearing the same expression on their faces, with their heads tilted in the same direction. They also finished each other's sentences. Eerie.

At the table next to Edie's sat a cowboy. Normally it would be surprising to have a cowboy in one's class, except that this cowboy had been in all of Edie's classes, so by ninth period she expected to see him. He wore brown boots, chaps, a vest, and a wide-brimmed hat. A magnificent mustache that curled up at the tips decorated his upper lip. This was Sam Blackmoore, the only student Edie didn't recognize from Horsemouth Middle School. Perhaps he recently moved to town. She'd have to find out more about him, but her first impression was that he was a major nutter, crazier than Jory, if that was even possible. Either that or he was incredibly stupid. What other reason could there be for wearing a Halloween costume on the first day of school? Sitting next to Sam was Victoria. The scowl on Victoria's face made it very clear that she did not enjoy sitting next to a rootin' tootin' cowboy.

Suddenly the door opened and in walked a thin man wearing thick round spectacles that magnified his eyes. He had a weak, almost nonexistent chin, so that his lower lip made a smooth slope to his clavicle, interrupted only by the large lump of his Adam's apple. He took his place behind the podium at the front of the room, lightly rubbing his long fingers together like a praying mantis.

"Good afternoon, class," he said in a high, reedy voice. "My name is Mister. Mr. Mister. I know it's an unusual name, but please don't make fun of it. This is Journalism One-A. If you didn't sign up for this elective, now is the time to excuse yourself." Nobody moved. Mr. Mister nodded thoughtfully. "All right, all right, it looks like everyone who is supposed to be here is here, or at least everyone who is not supposed to be here is not here. Has everyone been enjoying their first day of school?" Mr. Mister attempted a smile, which seemed a great effort on his part.

"No name game!" the students sang back in a messy sort of unison.

"I'm sorry, you'll all have to speak louder. I'm wearing earplugs." Mr. Mister adjusted his glasses. "I'm sensitive to loud noises. My nerves can't tolerate that . . . that cannon. Or the gong."

Jory raised his hand but didn't wait to be called on. "Why do you work at a school called Kaboom Academy if you can't stand loud noises?"

"I don't know where you got the idea that I can't handle boys. I can handle boys, boys and girls. That's one of the reasons I'm such an effective teacher. Now let's get down to business. In this class you are going to learn how to write and produce a newspaper. You will be taught how to find a story, how to research it, how to interview people for it, how to write it, how to edit it, and how to lay out the copy once it has been written. Simply put, you are going to understand what it is to be a journalist. We in this class have the profound responsibility of informing the students, faculty, administrators, staff, your parents, yea verily the entire Horsemouth community, about everything that is newsworthy at this institution. Our goal is to report those things that would be important to our readers without bias and with perfect accuracy."

Muffled laughter escaped from the students who thought Mr. Mister's use of "yea verily" was pompous. Victoria, unfazed by the archaic language, raised her hand.

"What about the opinion page? That would be biased," she pointed out.

"You'll have to wait to use the bathroom until class is over. You really should take care of that during lunchtime." Mr. Mister clapped his hands together. "Now. Our newspaper needs a name. Any suggestions?" As ideas were called out, Mr. Mister wrote them on the board. When he was finished, the list looked like this:

Cow Broom Crown Uncle
Dairy Die Mice
Boo Boo Bull Time

Pig Scoot
Antlers Do Best Westerns

"These are horrible suggestions," muttered Mr. Mister, shaking his head, his fingers fluttering to his neck, searching for the chin that wasn't there. "Downright awful. Seventh graders, are you? I expected better."

Jory rose from his seat, jogged to the front of the class, and picked up a marker from the whiteboard. Next to the suggestions he wrote:

Cow Broom Crown Uncle = KABOOM CHRONICLE
Dairy Die Mice = DAILY DYNAMITE
Boo Boo Bull Time = BOOM BOOM BULLETIN
Pig Scoot = BIG SCOOP
Antlers Do Best Westerns = ANSWERS TO
TEST QUESTIONS. THIS ONE WAS A JOKE, TO
GET KIDS TO READ THE NEWSPAPER. GET IT?
YOU CAN'T HEAR WHAT WE'RE SAYING!!!!!

Mr. Mister read what Jory had written and nodded. "Oh. I see. Thanks for clearing things up. Yes, these suggestions are much better. Much better indeed! Well, now that we have our list, let's take a vote."

After several minutes of vigorous debate, passionate entreaties, and a few death threats from Ruben, the class reached a consensus. Everyone liked *Daily Dynamite* the best, for it said everything they hoped the paper would be, mainly explosive. However, there were some obvious problems.

"We can't write a daily paper," Leo pointed out. "We don't have the manpower."

"You got that right. I am not putting in any extra time," Ruben said with a yawn.

"But calling it just *Dynamite* . . . ," began Aliya.

". . . is confusing," ended Taliya. "People may think . . ."

". . . it's a magazine about explosives."

"It's more confusing for a newspaper that calls itself the *Daily Dynamite* to only come out four times a year," Victoria said.

Margo leaped to her feet, waving her hand. "Ooh! Ooh! Guys! I've got it! Why don't we call it the *Dynamite Daily*?"

"That still has the word 'daily' in it," Victoria growled, leaving out the words "you nitwit," though that message came through loud and clear. Margo sat down and silently beat her forehead with her fist.

Jory jogged to the front of the room again, grabbed a whiteboard marker, and put an asterisk next to the *Daily Dynamite*. Then underneath in smaller letters, he wrote, **A Quarterly Periodical*. For a moment there was silence, broken only when the cowboy emitted a low whistle.

"By gum, I think that's gonna work just fine," the cowboy drawled. Everyone except Victoria joined in with approving comments.

"I think it's stupid, but far be it from me to disagree with the wisdom of the lowest common denominator," Victoria said sarcastically. Since nobody understood what she meant, it went by without comment. Then Ruben ran to the board, chose a red marker, and quickly drew a cartoon picture of a stick of dynamite with a sparkling fuse. With a few deft strokes he'd created the banner illustration for the paper and the school mascot.

"Splendid! Excellent!" said Mr. Mister, tapping his fingertips together. "Now all we have to do is divvy up the work. There are many jobs on a newspaper, and there will be plenty for everyone to do, but we need a leader. Who wants to be editor in chief?"

Aliya Naji raised her hand. "I thought you . . ."

". . . were the editor in chief," Taliya finished.

"The buses won't arrive until three o'clock. We've still got plenty of time," Mr. Mister assured them. "Now this is supposed to be a student-run paper. The more you do yourselves, the more you'll learn and the more pride you'll take in what you're doing."

"What he really means is that he'd rather let us do all the work while he plays games on his computer," Ruben said. Everyone laughed. It wasn't that funny but no one wanted to get on Ruben's bad side. Getting on Ruben's bad side meant being tripped in the hall, having your lunch flipped over, or ending up being shoved inside a locker, so everyone always laughed at even Ruben's most tepid jokes. Because of the earplugs, Mr. Mister couldn't hear Ruben. All he saw was the entire class opening their mouths and holding their sides and jerking. He wasn't sure what it meant.

"Er, *gesundheit,*" Mr. Mister said. "Anyway, the editor in chief must coordinate assignments among the reporters, read their stories and give suggestions on improvements, decide how the stories will be organized on the page, and answer any letters to the editor. Does anybody want this thankless job?"

Victoria's hand shot up like a rocket. It accelerated so quickly it broke the sound barrier, creating an isolated sonic boom right in the classroom. Regardless of the hardships, she knew that being the editor in chief of the school newspaper would look fantastic on her resume. Edie's hand was up next. What better way to know everything that was going on in the school than to be the editor in chief? The third person to raise his hand was Jory, who looked like he might just be stretching.

"All right, three people," Mr. Mister said. "Let's hear some speeches. I want each one of you to tell us what your qualifications are for being editor in chief."

Though she had not been asked to do so, Victoria strolled to the front of the room, her long braid swinging saucily behind her.

"I think you should vote for me because I have an IQ of a hundred and fifty," Victoria said. "I read at a college level, and I've read more books than everyone in this room combined. I don't need to use a computer to spot spelling or grammatical errors. I own a red pen, and I'm not afraid to use it. I feel comfortable ordering people around, and if you don't do the job well, I'm perfectly capable of fixing your mess. With me in charge the paper will get done and get done well. That's it."

Victoria took her seat to

scattered polite applause. "Edie, you're next," Mr. Mister said. Since Victoria had set the precedent of speaking from the front of the classroom, Edie followed suit.

"Hello, everyone, I'm the infamous Edie Evermint. Yes, the very same Edie Evermint who last year got two teachers fired at Horsemouth Middle School, wrecked eight close friendships, and spurred ten nervous breakdowns. How did I accomplish those things, you might ask? I'm an expert at gathering information," Edie explained proudly. "I've got an eye for detail, for smelling smoke and finding fires. I'm not held back by scruples or ethics either. I can direct this paper into being the juiciest gossip rag that has ever hit this sleepy town. This is what I do, people: I'm the Michelangelo of muckraking, the Shakespeare of scandal, the Galileo of gossip, the Babe Ruth of rumor mongering, the Einstein of exposé, the Mother Teresa of tittle-tattle! Well, Mother Teresa doesn't quite fit the picture, but you get what I mean. You want some excitement? You want a paper that people will want to read? Vote for Edie!"

Edie made her way back to her table to the stunned silence of the classroom.

"Thank you, Edie, very compelling," said Mr. Mister, who hadn't heard a word of her speech. "Jory, you're up."

Jory didn't go to the front of the class, choosing instead to stand at his seat. His speech was short. "I'm easy to talk to, I'm fair, and I'm not going to bust you if you're late with an article," he said. "I'll just help you get it done. And seriously, guys, are we really going to let the girls run things? Come on." He sat down.

Mr. Mister told everyone to write the name of the

person they were voting for on a piece of paper and put it in the shoe box he was passing around. After collecting the votes and counting them, he announced that Jory Bellard would be this year's editor in chief. Victoria simmered angrily. She was certain that the only reason she had lost was that she and Edie had split the girl vote and that all the boys had voted in solidarity for Jory. In fact, many of the girls had voted for Jory, impressed by his friendly, easygoing manner. Nevertheless, Victoria abruptly pushed herself away from the table and stormed out of the room, slamming the door behind her.

Edie took the news more gracefully, mainly because she also had voted for Jory. Once she'd thought about it, she realized that she didn't really want to be in charge; she wanted to be right there in the grime, digging up the dirt. Her new goal was to find the most shocking, jaw-dropping story of the year. But what would it be?

The cannon went off. The first day of school was over.

LESSON 1: WHAT MAKES A GOOD STORY?

The next day Mr. Mister divided up the rest of the newspaper responsibilities. Predictably, Ruben was awarded the position of sports editor. Margo was given the topic of student life. Sam would be responsible for puzzles, games, and comics. Victoria, Aliya and Taliya, and Edie would be the paper's investigative reporters. The good news was that Mr. Mister had removed one of his earplugs so that he could hear the students more clearly. It made the whole class run much more smoothly.

"We still need a photographer," Mr. Mister announced after looking over the list. "Leo, why don't you be the photographer? Do you know how to use a camera?"

"Yes, Mr. Mister," Leo said hesitantly, "but I don't think I'm a good choice for photographer. It's all explained in my file." Indeed, Leo's file had a long description about his condition. Leo struggled with extremely poor vision. Whereas a normal person might be able to see an object clearly from two hundred feet away, Leo had to be no more than twenty feet away. He didn't need a Seeing Eye dog or a cane and he didn't have to read using Braille, but his vision was seriously impaired.

"I read your file," Mr. Mister said, shaking his head. "Young man, you can't let something like this hold you back. I know you think being the photographer would be a challenge for you."

"Yes," agreed Leo. "It would be almost impossible."

"Now, don't be so negative. Challenges build character. I think you'll surprise yourself. I bet once you put your mind to it, you'll rise to the occasion and do a fantastic job. It's not going to be easy, though."

"No, sir, it won't. . . ."

"You're going to have to work at it. Work hard. Give it one hundred percent."

"Yes, sir, but—"

"But you can do it. I've got faith in you. You've got guts. I can see it in your eyes. Maybe you didn't know this, but the eyes are windows to the soul. Even though yours are a little crossed, I can see you've got what it takes to succeed at whatever you strive for. Don't let anyone tell you differently."

Leo felt a little light-headed. Nobody had ever had this much confidence in him before. It made him a little giddy. "I . . . I guess I can do my best," Leo said. He felt like he was jumping off a cliff.

"Good man. I like your can-do attitude. I'll issue you the camera at the end of class."

Leo floated back to his seat, slightly dazed, feeling

wonderfully pumped up. What he didn't know was that Mr. Mister needed to get a new prescription for his own thick glasses. He had misread "legally blind" as "legally blond." Mr. Mister thought Leo felt his blondness was holding him back. His whole speech was to assure Leo that despite the blond jokes, blonds are not dumb and that the color of his hair should make no difference in his performance. It was probably better that Leo didn't know about Mr. Mister's mistake. Mr. Mister clapped his hands together.

"All right, now that we've gotten the housekeeping taken care of, let's learn a little about how to find a story. Before you can write it, you first have to know what makes a story. What is news? Well, news is simply information about recent events or recent developments of events that would be of interest to people. Sometimes people don't recognize something as news because they don't realize it's something in which they *should* be interested. For that reason, it is important for a story to draw people in," Mr. Mister explained. "The first few sentences should hook the reader. For instance, let's say we wanted to write about the school auditorium catching fire. . . ."

"Oh my God!" gasped Margo. "The auditorium is on fire?"

"Why didn't . . . ," Aliya squealed.

". . . the alarm go off?" Taliya squeaked. The three girls scrambled to the window to try to catch a glimpse of the flames.

"I thought I smelled smoke, dagnabbit!" said the old prospector, snapping his suspenders. The old prospector had replaced the cowboy from yesterday. He wore jeans, boots, a flannel shirt with rolled-up sleeves, a felt hat, and a scruffy beard. It was an impressive disguise, but everyone was pretty sure it was Sam.

"No, no, I'm just giving an example of how you might write a story if the auditorium *were* to catch fire," Mr. Mister shouted above the excited chatter. "Take your seats, please! Leo, what are you doing at the whiteboard?"

"I thought I was looking out the window."

"The window's over here," Jory said, leading Leo to it. "But you can't see anything."

"That's because there's nothing to see," Victoria said.

"Not from this angle, anyway," Jory agreed. "I think I can see a little better from out here. . . ." Jory climbed out onto the ledge.

"How are we going to have school meetings without an auditorium?" Edie moaned. "Where will we put on performances? I hope we won't have to resort to using the cafeteria."

"I bet they roll in some of those trailers," Leo said. "The kind they set up when there's a hurricane or an earthquake."

"I hate those things. They smell like wet socks, by gum!" the old prospector railed, shaking his fist.

"Please! Class! You are overreacting!" Mr. Mister tried to shout above the fray, but his reedy voice was easily ignored.

"I don't know if anybody cares, because I know I don't, but Jory is standing on the ledge outside the window," Victoria announced.

"Jory! No!" Aliya yelled.

"Don't jump!" Taliya hollered in the exact same tone as her sister. The twins reached out the window and pulled him inside.

"I'm not going to jump . . . not this time. I'm not wearing a squirrel suit," Jory said.

"What's a squirrel suit?" Margo asked.

"It's an outfit made of parachute material with cloth between the legs and under the arms to give more surface area to the body. People use them for skydiving and base jumping. It allows you to fly like a flying squirrel!"

"Flying squirrels don't fly, they glide," Victoria corrected him.

"Why are we all just sitting here like jerks? We've got to do something!" Ruben shouted, racing from the classroom. Moments later the fire alarm sounded and Ruben returned. Jory gave him a fist bump for his quick thinking.

Mr. Mister held his head in his hands as though he were trying to keep it from splitting apart. He had given up. "All right, class, let's line up quickly and march out to the courtyard."

As the students formed a line, Victoria sidled up to Mr. Mister and tugged on his sleeve.

"I have your headline, Mr. Mister," Victoria said drily. "'*Big Dumb Student Sets False Alarm, Idiots Follow Stupidly.*'"

"Well, it's a bit long for a headline," Mr. Mister said. "And a little opinionated."

"I'll work on it." Victoria followed the line out the door.

"I want everybody to try to find a story to report on. That's your homework assignment!" Mr. Mister called out.

Nobody was surprised the next day when Victoria was the first one to hand in an article.

VICTORIA'S STORY

Bite Your Books

By VICTORIA ZACARIAS

Everyone knows that people take pills for many things: colds, headaches, vitamins, even bad breath. But a pill for information? This Monday students at Kaboom Academy were surprised to discover that instead of receiving hardcover books, or even digital books, they would instead receive them in pill form.

One of the many teaching tools created by child development and education expert Dr. Marcel S. Kaboom, the pills were designed so that students would not have to waste time reading.

"Nobody likes the process of reading," explained seventh-grade English teacher Mrs. Silverstrini. "It tires out your eyes, you can't find a comfortable position, and you keep losing your place. Dr. Kaboom realized it's not the words on the page that are important, but the ideas those words convey. He has developed a faster and more efficient way to absorb them!"

Students were at first unsure about taking books orally but gradually warmed up to the concept. Sixth grader Dillon Bourke liked the idea, pointing out that it will cut down on homework, leaving more time for extracurricular activities. Eighth grader Chad Bradley reminded others that things could be worse. "At least it's not a suppository," he remarked.

First period, seventh-grade English. Mrs. Silverstrini waited for the sound of the gong to die down before speaking. "Good morning, everyone! Settle down, please!" After she got the students' attention, Mrs. Silverstrini continued. "I'd like to go over the books we'll be covering this semester. We'll be starting with *The Hobbit,* J.R.R. Tolkien's masterpiece. It follows the adventures of Bilbo Baggins in the fantasy world of Middle Earth. Then we'll move on to *20,000*

Leagues Under the Sea, Jules Verne's classic about a couple of men held prisoner by the mysterious Captain Nemo. And as we head into the holiday season, we'll finish up with Charles Dickens's *A Christmas Carol,* a fable about stingy Ebenezer Scrooge and his strange visitation by three ghosts."

Mrs. Silverstrini headed to her desk, but suddenly she turned on her heel. "Whoops! I almost forgot! We'll also be covering *A Wrinkle in Time, Fahrenheit 451, A Separate Peace, Moby-Dick, Huckleberry Finn, Call of the Wild, The Yearling, The Red Badge of Courage,* and *To Kill a Mockingbird.*"

The students were appalled. "How can you expect us to get through all those books before winter break?" Leo complained. With his visual problems he had trouble getting through one book, let alone . . . how many was that? He counted on his fingers and gasped. "That's twelve books!"

Mrs. Silverstrini frowned. "Twelve? My goodness, I'm so sorry. Where is my head? I meant to include *Hound of the Baskervilles,* which is a marvelous Sherlock Holmes story, and my favorite classic tale of heroism, *The Odyssey.*" Now it was her turn to count on her fingers. When she was finished she nodded, satisfied. "Fourteen books in fourteen weeks. Perfect."

The tremendous groans emanating from the classroom rattled the lockers in the hallway. Only Victoria looked unperturbed.

"Oh my God," Margo said, eyes wide. "We are not going to have any time to do anything else!"

"Mrs. Silverstrini, we love reading . . . ," Aliya started.

". . . it's our favorite hobby, after doubles tennis, that is . . . ," Taliya continued.

". . . and we both read at a high school level . . . ," Aliya bragged.

". . . but even we think this is asking way too much!" Taliya concluded.

"Who said anything about reading?" Mrs. Silverstrini said slyly. She crossed to her desk and opened a small cardboard box on which was stamped KABOOM BOOKS. From the box she removed several packets; then she started moving up and down the aisles, handing them out. "These are book pills," she said matter-of-factly. "Developed by Dr. Kaboom, they are a quick and efficient way to consume books, and don't worry, they are one hundred percent safe. Go ahead, open them up!"

The students opened their packets. Inside were fourteen pills, each a different color. They were shaped like little books. Under every pill was stamped the title of the book as well as the author's name and the publisher.

Edie peered at them warily. "What the heck are book pills?"

"They're exactly what they sound like. Books in pill form. You simply pop out whichever book you want to consume, swallow it, and within five minutes it will be as if you've read the book. You'll know the plot, the characters, the dialogue and descriptions, everything."

"Whoa, that's . . . that's awesome!" Ruben said.

"Indeed, it is an incredible breakthrough in edumechanics," Mrs. Silverstrini agreed. "Go ahead, give it a try. The first book we'll be taking is *The Hobbit*. If you look at your packet it's the light pink pill at the top, on the far left, right over the words 'The Hobbit.' Now, just press on it, hard, and it should pop right through the foil on the other side."

"Who were they tested on?" Jory had already removed the *Hobbit* pill and was sniffing it suspiciously.

"Volunteers," Mrs. Silverstrini answered brightly. "Their parents signed a legally binding agreement with a non-litigation clause. That means if something goes wrong, they can't sue."

Victoria frowned. "Wait a minute, are you saying that *we* are the test subjects?"

"I really can't elaborate without a lawyer present." Mrs. Silverstrini gave a little shrug, conveying that the situation was out of her hands.

"Ah, but what if we don't take the pills?" said Merlin, stroking his long silver beard. Though this was the first time anyone had seen the wizard, who was dressed in a deep purple robe covered in stars and a matching pointed velvet cap that covered the silvery hair cascading down his back, Merlin's eyes and height matched that of the cowboy and the old prospector.

"That's perfectly fine, Sam, I'm not going to force anyone to take them. That would be unconscionable. So here are the books in hardcover." Mrs. Silverstrini bent over and lifted a large stack of books from the floor onto her desk. Then she bent over again and lifted up the rest of the books, placing them on the first stack, creating a wobbly tower. "You might have to make a couple of trips to get all these heavy books home. Good luck."

The students stared at the tower of books, then at the pills, then back at the tower of books. It was teetering dangerously. Mrs. Silverstrini noticed and straightened it up, which was difficult because the stack was taller than she was.

"Can we have some water?" said Ruben.

"They're chewable," said Mrs. Silverstrini.

"Then down the hatch," said Ruben, popping *The Hobbit* into his mouth. As he chewed, his face took on a thoughtful expression. "It tastes like . . . oatmeal with banana, brown sugar, butter, and a hint of cinnamon. . . . Hey, this is a really good book!"

The other students quickly followed suit, chewing eagerly. Immediately the classroom was filled with exclamations of surprise as the pills disintegrated on their tongues, filtering into their stomachs to be fully digested by their minds.

"I can't believe poor Bilbo has to go on this journey," Margo said with a laugh. "It's so against a hobbit's nature to be a hero."

"That's the point," Jory said. "He is an unlikely hero, but he rises to the occasion."

"Maybe it means that we all have the makings of a hero within us . . . ," Aliya said.

". . . and we only need the right circumstances for it to come out," said Taliya.

Victoria was the only one who hadn't swallowed *The*

Hobbit. That was because she had popped all the pills out and had forgotten which one it was. She knew it was pink, but there were four pills that were various shades of that color. Which one could it be?

"You know, Gollum's riddles really aren't that good," Ruben said. "I can come up with funnier riddles than that."

"Yes, you definitely can, because you're hilarious," Leo said, sucking up. "But these jokes aren't supposed to be funny, they're supposed to be brain twisters. It's like a battle of wits." Leo was overjoyed. For the first time in his life he had actually "read" a book without having to press it up to his nose. Dr. Kaboom was a genius.

Victoria was desperate. There was a book discussion going on and she had not yet contributed. Even Margo, who was spectacularly wrong 98 percent of the time, was looking more intelligent than she was. Even Ruben with his big dumb fat head was looking sharper. Victoria made a decision. She mashed the four pink pills together on a piece of paper, sweeping the powder into her hand to lick off.

The taste was horrible. She identified the oatmeal right away, but mixed into it was the spicy flavor of barbecue chicken and the unmistakable tang of tuna salad. A tinge of buttered popcorn was the final insult. At first she thought she was going to be sick, but she managed to choke it down.

"Look, the most important theme of the story is the question of Bilbo's development as a hero," Victoria began after clearing her throat. "When he starts the story he is timid, but all that changes when he confronts the ghost of Christmas Past."

"Wait . . . what ghost of Christmas Past?" Edie interrupted.

"The ghost! Surely that character hasn't escaped your notice." Victoria snorted. "Who do you think sends him on his quest down the Mississippi River with his escaped slave Moby-Dick? Hello?"

"And does Bilbo finish that quest?" Jory said slowly and carefully, as though he were speaking to a toddler or a maniac.

"Of course he does, *dummkopf*!" Victoria snapped sarcastically. "Even you must remember that great moment when Bilbo cries, 'God bless us, every one!' then twists his harpoon, becomes invisible, stabs Tom Sawyer, and gives Bob Cratchit a great big white whale for Christmas dinner. . . ."

A dead silence fell over the room, and Victoria slowly became aware that everyone was staring at her.

Margo broke the quiet. "Oh my God, you sound like me."

Immediately Victoria realized what had happened. All the characters and plots had gotten mixed up when she'd mashed the pills together. This was a major catastrophe. The class started to snicker. The snickers turned into chuckles, and then gales of laughter, rolling over each other like waves crashing on the shore. Suddenly the feeling of nausea returned.

"Excuse me!" Victoria squeaked as she raced out of the room. "I have to sneeze!"

Victoria flew down the hall and into the girls' bathroom, quickly pushing the stall doors open one by one to make sure nobody was in there with her. Once she confirmed that she was alone, she crumpled to the floor, hugging her knees as she started to bawl.

Drat! Why couldn't she stop this uncontrollable crying? She had been cursed with this hideous problem for as long as she could remember, and it was made worse by the fact that she was so perfect in everything else.

Early on, Victoria had been identified as academically gifted. She had learned to read sooner than everyone her age; she'd polished off an entire children's encyclopedia before she'd even begun kindergarten. She could multiply three-digit numbers in her head and beat any adult in chess. Victoria's intelligence was not a great surprise to Victoria's mother and father, Gloria and Oswaldo Zacarias, who had already had a son and daughter who were just as gifted as Victoria. Carlos and Andrea were both in high school by the time Victoria was born, and they were attending impressive universities by the time she was four, so Victoria did not get to know them very well. She grew up more like an only child, but with the knowledge that her siblings had set the bar very high and that she was expected to perform academically as well as they did.

Victoria exceeded expectations. Once she started school, she flourished. In no time at all, it was obvious that she knew more than her teachers, and she wasn't too afraid or polite to prove it. For a teacher, having Victoria Zacarias in your class meant certain humiliation. It meant feeling inadequate five days a week. That is, if the teacher even showed up five days a week. Teachers who had Victoria in their class took more sick days on average than other teachers. Some of them were driven to drink.

Eventually the Zacariases pulled Victoria out of public school to instruct her at home instead. Everybody thought it was because Victoria was so incredibly smart . . . but they were wrong. The reason Victoria no longer attended public school was because of her embarrassing personality quirk: she was a great big crybaby.

The first time it happened was at the start of kindergarten. Victoria was three years old, two years younger than most of the other children. That day, the kindergarten teacher had brought a special treat: Popsicles! Victoria's favorite color was blue. She wanted a blue raspberry Popsicle, but instead she received a red cherry Popsicle. She stared at the red Popsicle, refusing to eat it, watching it drip, drip, drip onto the carpet.

"Why don't you eat your Popsicle, Victoria?" Mrs. Lewinsky asked kindly.

"I wanted a blue Popsicle," Victoria answered.

"I know, but we ran out of blue Popsicles," Mrs. Lewinsky said.

"But that's what I wanted." Victoria's lip quivered. She sensed that she was losing the argument.

"I know, sweetie, but you can't always have what you want. You get what you get and you don't get upset."

Victoria's throat tightened. She couldn't breathe. And suddenly, before she could do anything about it, tears burst from her eyes, spouting from her ducts like water from a broken sprinkler head. She could do nothing to stop it. Mrs. Lewinsky had to call Mrs. Zacarias and have her take Victoria home. Both women chalked it up to immaturity; after all, three is awfully young to be in kindergarten, regardless of how smart you are.

But it didn't stop. First grade. Second grade. Third grade. Victoria never grew out of it. By fourth grade she knew she was far beyond the age at which crying over minor disappointments would be considered appropriate. But she couldn't control herself. As soon as somebody refused to give her what she wanted, or whenever she got the answer to a question wrong, on went the waterworks. Generally Victoria avoided making a scene by studying so hard that she simply got everything right. Her perfection intimidated people, and for that reason she always got her way. Problem solved.

As time went on that strategy fell apart. Once her peers matured, they lost their sense of fear and awe. They challenged Victoria just to annoy her, and even though she knew they were only teasing, the result was the same. As soon as she felt that pressure building against her tear ducts, she had to manufacture some excuse and make a quick getaway. This disappearing act started to take its toll. Classmates spread rumors that the reason Victoria rushed out of the room was because she had an intestinal problem. That was almost worse than having a reputation as a crybaby. The situation was quickly becoming a disaster.

After she finished fifth grade, Victoria's parents decided to let her stay home the following year and take courses online. That worked for a while, but then Victoria's parents got divorced. Now Mrs. Zacarias could no longer stay at home and monitor Victoria's studies; she had to work full-time. She didn't want her daughter spending the entire day in the house all by herself (or worse, spending the day running around the neighborhood), so she told Victoria she had to go back to school for seventh grade. They had both hoped that Kaboom Academy, with its progressive, experimental philosophy, might be the answer to Victoria's problem, but here she was hiding in the bathroom, face damp as a wash-rag, eyes a blistering red, so apparently it wasn't.

A sudden noise interrupted Victoria's reverie, the sharp creak of a hinge turning. Victoria spun around in time to see the bathroom door close. Great. Just great. She dragged herself to the sink to splash some water on her face and felt a twinge in her stomach. Ugh. These books were not sitting well.

Her stomach lurched and the bitter taste of bile, oatmeal, tuna, and barbecue chicken—with a tinge of popcorn—hit her throat.

She dove into one of the stalls and leaned over the toilet. *The Hobbit, Moby-Dick, Huckleberry Finn,* and *A Christmas Carol,* as well as some orange juice and Cheerios from breakfast, erupted from Victoria's throat. She heaved again, and the last bits of plot, character, themes, and symbols from the four classics poured out of her.

Victoria sighed and sat back on her heels, feeling much better. Thank goodness she'd gotten sick; it was the perfect excuse for her strange behavior. Victoria headed to the nurse's office, a skip in her step.

Problem solved.

LESSON 2: THE FIVE Ws

PHOTO BY LEO REISS

"Let's get down to the nuts and bolts of writing a story." Mr. Mister stood at the front of the classroom and wrote on the whiteboard. "Every news story has to answer five questions. Those questions are *Who? What? When? Where?* and *Why?* We call them the five Ws." Standing back from the board where he had written the words, Mr. Mister pointed to each one as he went through them. "*Who* is the article about? *What* is the issue? *When* did it happen? *Where* did it happen? And finally, *why* did it happen?"

Margo raised her hand. "Yes, Margo?"

"What about *Which?*"

"What about which what?"

"Not which what, just *Which?*"

"I'm not following."

"'Which' is a question word," Margo explained.

"They're all question words. Which do you want to discuss?"

"Exactly. 'Which' is the one I want to discuss."

Mr. Mister was starting to get a headache. "I think we're talking in circles here, Margo. Which word do you want to talk about?"

"'Which.'"

"Yes. Which?"

"Right."

"You have questions about which word?"

"Yes."

"Okay, just ask the question," Mr. Mister said, losing his patience.

"'Which' begins with a 'W'—" Margo began.

"They all do," Mr. Mister interrupted. "That's why they're called the five Ws."

"But they could be six Ws, if you included *Which?*"

"How am I supposed to know which?"

"Well, *How?* is another one, Mr. Mister, that's a very good point, though it doesn't start with a 'W.' But I was talking about *Which?*"

"I don't know! I don't know which! I wish you would tell me!" Mr. Mister was now looking forward to the cannon explosion that would mark the end of the class, but that wouldn't happen for thirty-five minutes. Most of the students seemed to have fallen into a stupor, lost in their own personal daydreams. Ruben's head was flung back, his mouth was open, and a loud snore was sawing through the conversation. Aliya and Taliya had started playing a card game. The only one paying any attention at all, besides Margo, was Abraham Lincoln, who nodded slowly, stroking his beard. The bright blue eyes peering out from under the stovepipe hat clued Mr. Mister to the fact that Abe Lincoln was, of course, Sam Blackmoore.

"You. Sam, isn't it?" Mr. Mister said.

"I beg to differ, sir, but my name is Abraham Lincoln. You are addressing the seventeenth president of the United States. . . ."

"Sixteenth," growled Victoria.

"Sixteenth. I'm not so good at sums and such." Abe Lincoln chuckled.

"Oh, for heaven's sake," snapped Victoria. "Do some research!"

"I saved the Union," Lincoln continued unperturbed, but he was interrupted by Mr. Mister.

"Yes, yes, thank you for that. Do you know what she's talking about?" Mr. Mister said, pointing at Margo.

"Yes indeed, I do, sir," Abe Lincoln said, rising to his feet and clearing his throat. "Four score and seven years ago, this young lady raised a question of great significance. . . ."

"'Four score and seven' means 'eighty-seven,' you know," Victoria muttered loudly enough for everyone to hear.

Abe Lincoln continued unruffled. "This fine young lady sought to find out why the word 'which' was not included among the other W words for the purposes of writing a newspaper article. As you probably know, sir, the word 'which' is often used when asking the type of question where one must choose between two or more options, and it also begins with a 'W,' so it would fit in nicely with the other question words that begin with the letter 'W.'" Mr. Lincoln smiled at the appreciative Margo and took his seat.

"Thank you, Mr. President."

"It was my pleasure."

"So what's the answer to the question?" Leo said.

"I don't really have a good answer," Mr. Mister admitted. "But if you find reason to answer the question 'which' or even 'how,' for that matter, go right ahead and do it."

"Thank you!" Margo said gratefully. She turned to Abraham Lincoln. "And thank you for freeing the slaves!" For once Margo hadn't made a complete fool of herself, and she had the sixteenth president of the United States to thank for that.

RUBEN'S STORY

PHOTO BY LEO REISS

Danger Ball

By RUBEN CHAO

Dodgeball: too dangerous or not dangerous enough? Over the past few years, the game of dodgeball has come under scrutiny. Many schools have banned it, fearing it has become just one more opportunity for bullies to target and pound weaker kids. Dr. Kaboom, "Hot Mustard" at Kaboom Academy, has

a different belief.

"It's true that bullies have hijacked this wonderful game," Coach Freeman said in an interview. "That is why Dr. Kaboom has taken the action out of the students' hands and put it where it belongs: in the hands of the balls. Yes, I'm aware that balls don't have hands, but that's beside the point. Dr. Kaboom has designed a unique style of dodgeball that has revolutionized the game by making it evenly matched."

Seventh grader Riley Estabrook, the frequent target of bullies in the past, likes the new version of the game. "It's harder to play but it's more fair. It used to be that the weaker kids got slammed. Now everyone gets hurt."

Fourth period, physical education, more commonly known as PE. The students had changed into shorts, T-shirts, and athletic shoes. The girls stood on one side of the gym, the boys on the other. They might have mingled when they were in fifth grade, or maybe even sixth, but now that they were in seventh grade, the girls had become very self-conscious, and none of them was looking forward to exercising in front of the boys. The majority only cared about how they looked, and had spent a considerable amount of time in front of a mirror getting ready for school that morning. Forty-five minutes of running around and sweating would certainly ruin their hard work.

The boys, on the other hand, barely noticed what they

looked like when they left the house. More than once some boy had come to school wearing two different socks. One even arrived with his pajama bottoms on under his jeans. The only boy who did care what he looked like was Sam. Today he looked like a pirate.

Coach Freeman entered the gym carrying a large net bag filled with red rubber balls. "Hello, everyone, good morning," he said brightly. The students returned the greeting.

"Coach Freeman, why do guys and girls have to take PE at the same time?" complained Edie as she collected her strawberry-blond hair into a ponytail and wrapped it in an elastic band.

"Because the school is so new there are only twenty seventh graders," Coach Freeman explained. "Ten boys and ten girls. There aren't enough students to fill out two teams."

"What about basketball?" Ruben suggested. "There are five people on each team. You could make two boy teams and two girl teams."

"I don't know how to play basketball," admitted Coach Freeman.

"There's also volleyball," Ruben spoke up again, "with six people on each team, but you can easily play with five."

"I don't know how to play volleyball either," said the coach.

"How about calisthenics?" Leo suggested. "You know, jumping jacks, push-ups, stomach crunches." Everyone groaned.

"Belay that idea, ye bilge rat!" growled the pirate.

Ruben seconded that motion with a hard shove to Leo's shoulder, sending Leo stumbling into the bleachers.

Leo didn't like calisthenics either, but it was practically the only athletic activity he could do. For him team sports were a disaster. Having a legally blind person on your team was a huge liability. But it didn't matter; the coach rejected Leo's suggestion as well.

"I don't know how to do calisthenics," confessed Coach Freeman.

"Are you a real coach or do you just play one on TV?" Ruben joked, though there was an element of seriousness to the question. His classmates dutifully laughed anyway, some going a little overboard, wiping tears from their eyes and slapping their knees.

"I'm not a real coach," Coach Freeman answered. "I'm your bus driver, Ivan. I guess you haven't recognized me with the coach's cap and the whistle."

Now that he had mentioned it, the students did recognize Ivan. It wasn't that the cap and whistle made him look that much different, it was just that in all the excitement of starting a new school, none of them had thought to take a good look at the bus driver.

"So what can we possibly play together?" Victoria said. "The guys are going to be too rough no matter what sport we choose."

"Shiver me timbers, lassie! Not all these scurvy dogs be rough," growled the pirate, waving the hook that replaced his hand. "Ye be making sweeping generalizations."

"You're an idiot. You do know that, don't you?" countered Victoria.

"Arrrgh," the pirate said sadly.

"I may not be a real coach," Coach Freeman said, "but I have been trained to teach you a brand-new game: dodgeball!"

"All right! Yeah!" Ruben crowed. Dodgeball was Ruben's favorite. He was an expert at hurling balls with the accuracy of a sharpshooter, knocking weaker, awkward kids down like bowling pins.

"Dodgeball isn't . . . ," Aliya began.

". . . a new game," Taliya said, finishing the scoff. "It's been around . . ."

". . . since cavemen threw . . ."

". . . rocks at each other." The two sisters tittered at their drawn-out joke.

"It's not the game that's new, it's the Kaboom Method of playing the game," Coach Freeman announced.

"Well, I guess we have to break up into teams," Margo said with a shrug. "What's it going to be, boys against the girls or girls against the boys?" Everyone just looked at her. Margo could've sworn she heard the distinct sound of somebody slapping their forehead in disbelief. She knew it was Victoria.

"Let's pick captains!" Ruben suggested. "I'll be one, and . . ." He looked around to see who he would least want on his team. It came down to Leo or Margo. Leo couldn't see anything, but Margo would probably throw the ball at her own teammates. "Margo, you can be the other one."

"No, no, no. You don't understand," Coach Freeman interrupted. "You are all on the same team. Instead of battling against each other, you will be helping each other."

"Against who?" the kids said in unison.

"The *balls*."

Coach Freeman opened the neck of the net bag, grabbing the bottom to shake out the balls, which rolled onto the floor. All together there were twelve. They looked like traditional red kickballs, but looks can be deceiving.

"Wow, these balls have bounce!" Ruben remarked. Indeed, the balls seemed to bounce higher than might be expected of balls that had just been released from a bag. In fact, the height and intensity of the bounces seemed to increase with every impact, defying the laws of physics. Then, in an astonishing move, the balls started to coordinate with each other, creating patterns like synchronized swimmers or a marching band. First they formed a circle, then a star, then a line of twelve, then two lines of six. They bounced in a syncopated beat with the precision of bongo drummers. Dancing balls! All the students gaped in awe. In their entire lives they had never seen anything like this.

"So how do we play?" Ruben asked eagerly, remembering the point of the demonstration.

"It's a very easy game," Coach Freeman answered. "These are the rules. Number one, you must stay in the gym. Number two, when the balls come at you, dodge them or catch them. Any ball you catch you can put back in the bag, and that ball is out. Number three, if you get hit, you're out, and you have to go to the prison, which is the bleachers. Number four, the only way you can get out of prison is if somebody makes it to the bleachers without getting hit. Then you can stage a prison break, and everyone who is in prison can come back onto the floor of the gym. Got it?"

The students shrugged. The rules did seem pretty easy.

"Can't we just watch the balls dance?" Everyone's favorite target, Margo did not care for dodgeball.

"No, the balls really aren't dancers," Coach Freeman said. "They brought their game face; let's see you bring yours. Okay! Are you guys ready?"

The students readied themselves, feeling a little foolish.

"Are you ready, balls?"

At this, the balls did something quite frightening. They immediately stopped bouncing and scooted into a straight line.

"Okay, one, two, three . . . *dodgeball!*" cried Coach Freeman, tweeting his whistle.

With each count the balls had bounced in unison, higher and higher and higher. *ONE* bounce. *TWO* BOUNCE. *THREE* B O U N C E. At the end of the count, the balls dive-bombed the students. The kids scattered, shouting and screaming. Those with quick reflexes succeeded in dodging the red rubber missiles by leaping out of the way or flattening themselves on the floor. Leo couldn't see the ball coming and was pounded squarely in the back. He hadn't expected to last very long, so he had stationed himself near the bleachers. Now that he was out, he nonchalantly climbed into the prison, sitting on the third-row bench.

What Leo hadn't expected was the purple ball. As soon as he sat down it appeared from underneath the seats, bouncing softly behind him on the fourth-row bench.

"Hey, Coach Freeman, what's this purple ball for—" Leo began, but before he could get to the question mark in his sentence, the ball leaped up and slammed him in the back of the head.

"Ow!"

"That's the prison guard."

"Prison guard? Why is there a prison guard?"

"It's a pretty feeble prison that doesn't have a prison guard." Coach Freeman chuckled. The purple ball slammed into Leo's head again.

"*Ouch!* Can you tell it to stop?"

"Don't be a poor sport, Leo, it's part of the game. It's just trying to get you to behave and sit quietly, with your hands in your lap."

"So if I sit quietly with my hands in my lap, I can get out early on good behavior?" The purple ball answered that question with a third slam to Leo's head.

Meanwhile, a war was raging on the floor of the gym. Balls zoomed through the air, chasing down their targets. Sometimes they worked in tandem: while one ball came from the front, the other came from the back, sweeping the unaware teen's feet out from under him. Aliya and Taliya made a very large target as they ran arm in arm around the gym. Two balls took them out at the same time, whamming the twins in their backs. The girls picked themselves up off the highly polished floor, turning just in time to see the balls celebrate by bouncing against each other in the air before heading off to look for other prey.

"Was that . . ."

". . . a chest bump? These balls are . . ."

". . . really arrogant!" They trudged over to the bleachers, where Margo, Victoria, and Sam the pirate had already joined Leo, as had several other seventh graders. Because nobody could sit still and everybody wanted to talk, they were at the mercy of the purple prison guard, which bounced from one head to another in its own personal game of Whac-a-Mole. Only five minutes into the game and the balls were clearly winning.

Jory and Ruben were the two students able to successfully avoid the onslaught. Because Jory enjoyed jumping from high places, he had lots of experience flinging himself around in ways normal human beings would consider foolhardy. He did so now, tossing himself about, leaping, diving, running up walls, and flipping to evade the balls. Ruben's skill was his quick hands. No matter how fast the balls came at him, he was able to catch them. He would then stuff them into the net bag, which was the only way they became officially out of play. It was while he was doing this that he discovered another interesting characteristic about the balls.

"These balls bite!" he yelled as he shook one off his finger back into the net bag. "That's not fair!"

"Really? They're not supposed to bite," Coach Freeman said. "Clearly that ball has a bad attitude."

"Not only that, it has teeth!" Some of the students laughed at this remark, while others tittered nervously, not quite sure if Ruben was making a joke. He wasn't.

"Hmm, I guess they would have to, wouldn't they? But they're not very sharp. No blood, right?" Coach Freeman didn't offer much consolation.

Seven minutes later, seventeen students were sitting in the prison, but thanks to Ruben's quick hands, there were only three balls left in play. Jory was more exhausted than he'd ever been in his life, having been in constant motion for close to fifteen minutes. And all of the diving and rolling and flipping was making him dizzy. The prisoners wanted to cheer on their classmates, but they were fearful of the very strict purple guard. Most of them had already been bonked in the head enough times that they didn't want to invite more punishment. All that bonking had also made them unobservant. If anyone had been paying close attention, they would have noticed that besides Jory and Ruben, there was one other student who had not gotten out and was not sitting in the prison bleachers, and that was Edie.

Because of her carefully honed eavesdropping skills, Edie had found a very good hiding place. She had entrenched herself within a rolled-up gymnastics mat about twenty feet from the bleachers and was biding her time, waiting for Ruben to do all the hard work and for Jory to tire himself out. She checked her watch. There were five more minutes to go. She could hear Jory springing off the wall in his effort to escape the balls and Ruben muttering under his breath every time a ball bit him, which was often. Apparently all of the balls had bad attitudes.

Sam had figured out that despite their ability to strategize, the balls could only bounce in a straight line; they could not change course in midair. You could predict the speed, direction, and arc of their bounce if you paid attention. The pirate decided that despite certain retribution, he would help his teammates.

"He be coming at you from behind, me hearty!" the pirate warned, then followed with a loud "Blast ye to smithereens, ye nasty beastie!" after the purple ball swiftly reprimanded him. Feeling sorry for Sam, others took up the duty of warning the two remaining students about which direction the balls were coming from. It didn't matter that Jory was nuts and Ruben was obnoxious; they were not only human beings but classmates, and the teens wanted them to win. This might not have been the case if they had been playing against cute little puppies, but these balls weren't cute little puppies. They were vicious and needed to be defeated. Edie heard all of this from the relatively safe confines of her hiding place.

Two minutes to go. The balls had come up with a wily strategy, picking the boys off one at a time. They first surrounded Jory, bouncing calmly in unison as he swiveled around, his eyes darting from one ball to the other. Then they fell upon him. In his wearied state there was simply nothing Jory could do to avoid them. He executed an amazing backflip-with-a-twist that would have been the envy of any Olympic gymnast, but the three balls overwhelmed him. After the pummeling, he dragged himself over to the bleachers for congratulations from his fellow students and some much-needed rest. Then the three balls turned their attention to Ruben.

Ruben backed away slowly as the balls rolled toward him. As with Jory, they quickly surrounded him. It appeared from their tiny bounces that they were aiming low, probably figuring that if they got near his hands, they would end up in the net bag. Then, as if a charge had been blown from a bugle, they attacked, zeroing in on Ruben's ankles. But instead of trying to scoop them up, Ruben surprised everyone by leaping straight into the air and executing an extraordinary pirouette: one, two, three times he spun around, his arms clasped around his body, his toes pointed. Edie watched from her hiding place and almost gasped, which would of course have been a terrible mistake. Meanwhile, the balls had already launched themselves, and since they couldn't change course, they met right where Ruben had been standing only moments before. They slammed against each other with such force that they exploded outward, hitting three different walls of the gym.

The students roared, standing to give Ruben a well-deserved ovation. Ruben bowed deeply, all the while keeping an eye on the balls as they regrouped in the far corner of the gym, apparently humiliated by their failure.

Ruben couldn't believe he had actually done that pirouette. Not that he hadn't known he could do it—of course he'd known that; after all, he'd been practicing it over and over and over again until it was nearly perfect. But he had never meant to do it in front of his classmates. It wasn't the sort of move you'd expect from a tough guy, and he had a reputation to uphold.

Ruben Chao had always been a big kid. When he was born he weighed twelve pounds. "You nearly killed me!" his mother liked to remind him. "It was like birthing a giraffe!" By the time he could walk, Ruben was already bigger than his sister, who was a year older than him. When he started first grade, he was the size of most third graders. By fifth grade Ruben was so tall people thought he was in high school. The summer before seventh grade he had another growth spurt. When he arrived on the first day of school, he towered over all of his teachers.

Being a guy of above-average height has its benefits, but there's nothing good about being a giant. The worst thing was that everyone assumed Ruben was older than he really was. They expected him to be smarter and more mature than a normal thirteen-year-old because they thought he was eighteen. They also figured he must have been held back because he was stupid. This led to the next assumption, that he was so stupid he didn't know his own strength and would run roughshod over smaller kids. Wary parents were forever shielding their children from him. But Ruben was the one who needed the shielding. Because of his size, kids treated him like a jungle gym. They would rush him, hit him, even climb on him, and he had to just stand there and take it or risk being labeled a bully.

The other bad thing about being big was that everyone

expected you to be strong, tough, and good at sports. Ruben did not particularly like sports. He was not going to like basketball no matter how many times his parents placed a ball in his hands. "You don't have to like it or even be good at it," his dad always said. "You'll have recruiters begging you to just sit on the bench and scare the other team." Ruben liked volleyball even less. And he hated football. But because he was so super-sized, he was better at those sports than his classmates. His reputation for being athletically gifted was completely false. He wasn't a jock; he was just huge. And he was getting fed up.

One day near the end of fifth grade, Ruben was at the park, minding his own business, when three second graders leaped on him and started climbing him, pretending he was Mount Everest. Ruben decided he'd had enough. Picking them off as if removing lint from a sweater, he tossed them carelessly to the ground. He didn't mean to hurt them, but a person falling from any height is bound to get a few cuts and scrapes. Sure enough, the kids got a little bloodied and reported that Ruben had "beat them up," an outrageous exaggeration. It didn't matter. His reputation was established.

At first Ruben was upset at being labeled a bully, but then he thought better of it. He was getting a lot more respect; nobody dared touch him or call him names. Kids gave him a wide berth. It meant that he didn't have any friends, but he'd never had friends prior to this, so that was an even trade. Every once in a while, he'd trip someone or give somebody a shove just to reinforce his status. He wasn't very happy, but at least people left him alone.

The only person who understood what Ruben was going through was his sister, Sally. She saw right through his bully persona; after all, he was a completely different person at home—sweet, gentle, and kind. She felt that living a double life was psychologically unhealthy and that Ruben needed to find his "authentic self." Sally subscribed to New Age spirituality and liked using the jargon because it made her feel smart. But like most people, Sally had a difficult time seeing beyond Ruben's athletic build.

"I don't understand why you don't like sports," Sally had ventured as they passed some kids playing a pickup game of basketball on their way home from Horsemouth Middle School. Ruben had just started sixth grade, and Sally was in seventh. She had already seen how kids avoided her brother and didn't want him to go through school a pariah. She thought that the bond created by playing on a team with other guys would solve his problems. "You're an energetic guy, you don't sit around watching TV or playing video games. And you're a great athlete. Most people like things that they're good at."

"Actually, I do like sports," Ruben had answered. "I enjoy being physical. I just don't like that 'rah-rah, we're number one, in your face' stuff. All that boasting makes me mad, even if I'm on the winning team. I'd rather just work on skills. Why do there have to be winners and losers anyway? I don't think there's anything fun about making people feel terrible."

After that conversation Sally started looking at her brother a little differently, and she noticed things she hadn't before. Yes, Ruben was built like a majestic redwood. Yes, he had superhero proportions. Yes, he had an enviable combination of muscle, power, speed, and brute force. But Ruben had even more. He had nimbleness and agility. Balance. Grace. Rhythm. Once Sally expanded her picture of her brother, she realized he had the raw materials of an excellent dancer.

Not long after that, Sally convinced Ruben to come with her to her dance class. It took three invitations, but finally he had gone reluctantly, agreeing only to watch, not to participate. He knew there were a few boys in her class but had imagined they'd be wearing frilly tutus and prancing around like idiots. He was wrong. There were only four boys, and they wore black leggings, white T-shirts, and black dance shoes, not much worse than what a guy would have to wear if he was on the wrestling team. After the boys and girls warmed up together, the boys split off into their own room. They had a rigorous, athletic workout with a male instructor, Eric, who was slender and slight but barked orders like a drill sergeant, commenting on each boy's form, style, and skills. Ruben liked him immediately.

Eric noticed Ruben's excitement. Sally had already told him about her brother, about his size and build, and so for several weeks Eric had been expecting him. Even though he had been warned, Ruben's size astounded him. How would he be able to instruct this boy? It would be like trying to teach a bull how to dance. Still, he invited Ruben to join them. Boy dancers were rare, and he wasn't about to dissuade any boy who had even a mild interest.

While Ruben changed into his PE clothes and slipped into a spare pair of dance shoes from the lost and found, the other boys snickered, joking about Ruben's size as he stretched to warm up. But when he started to dance with them, the snickers turned to shocked silence, then impressed murmurs. Not only was Ruben able to keep up with the others, but he had so much stamina and his limbs were so limber that he surpassed them. His leaps were higher; his poses more dramatic. He was a prodigy, a natural. The other boys looked at each other, realizing that he was out of their league. From now on it would be Ruben first and then the rest of them. But Ruben was so much fun to watch, they didn't care.

Once Ruben started dancing he became much happier. Thanks to Sally, he had found his "authentic self," and he had made friends with the other boys in the class. However, it didn't help his social situation at Horsemouth Middle School. Though there was certainly nothing wrong with ballet dancing, it was definitely an activity more often associated with girls. It would only invite more teasing among guys his age. Ruben decided not to tell anyone. Nobody needed to know what he did on Wednesday and Saturday afternoons. The dance shoes, the black leggings, and the white T-shirt that he kept stuffed in his backpack were his own little secret.

That was why the pirouette was problematic. He looked at his classmates in the bleachers. Sure, now they were cheering, but once they thought about it and figured out what it meant . . . then what? Fortunately for Ruben, they didn't have time to think. The purple ball was vigorously pounding their heads, infuriated by their rowdy team spirit. And now with only one more minute to go, the three red balls flew at Ruben with all the force they could muster, one at his feet, one at his head, and one at his chest. There was no escaping them, no place to duck, and no place to jump. This time it was Ruben who slammed against the wall, directly over the rolled-up mat where Edie was hiding. Or rather, where Edie *had been* hiding. She had left only moments before Ruben landed with a heavy thud on the thick padding.

Edie raced to the bleachers, bounding to the top, taking two steps at a time. "Guess what, everyone! You're all free! Prison break! Prison break!" she yelled. With a gleeful roar all the students leaped back to the gym floor. The purple ball bounced from one empty bleacher bench to another, seemingly unsure of what to do with itself.

Coach Freeman blew his whistle. "That's the game!" he announced.

"Yay! We win!" Edie shouted. The students erupted in joyful screams, high-fiving each other.

"Whoa, not so fast. Don't you think you were cheating?" Coach Freeman said.

"Nope. You didn't say we had to stay on the court, you said we had to stay in the gym, which I did. You didn't say anything about concealing yourself, which I also did. We won fair and square."

"You make a good argument," Coach Freeman agreed. "Students win, twenty to three."

Edie formed an "L" with her forefinger and thumb as she faced the three agitated balls that had just had their win stolen from under them, and waved it at them triumphantly. "Sorry, losers!"

"Losers! Losers! Losers!" chanted the students, making the same sort of "L" with their thumbs and forefingers and thrusting them at the balls.

The balls quivered. They shook. Then they completely lost it. It's not often that a person gets to see a ball lose its temper. Certainly none of these students had, and in truth, none of them would ever see it again. This was a special once-in-a-lifetime moment. They watched, fascinated, as the balls hurled themselves against the walls in a violent rage, ricocheting from one end of the gym to the other, the speed of their flight increasing from the force of their impact against the walls. Harder and harder they slammed; faster and faster they went. In a final burst of anger, the purple ball crashed through one of the windows near the ceiling, and the three free balls followed, soaring after it. The students heard the smacks from their landing outside, their bouncing sounds moving farther and farther away until they could hear nothing at all.

Coach Freeman sighed. "Those balls had a *very* bad attitude."

The cannon fired. Class was over.

ALIYA AND TALIYA'S STORY

PHOTO BY LEO REISS

New Form of Discipline

By ALIYA AND TALIYA NAJI

Kaboom Academy prides itself on its progressive philosophy, but like all schools, it has rules. Before any of us were allowed to attend, we had to sign the Kaboom Academy Honor Code. Many of you probably did not read it carefully because it was

so boring, but we did, and we can tell you that you did not miss much. It basically lists the rules of the school, exactly as you would think. Here they are again:

1. No cheating.
2. No stealing.
3. No damaging school property.
4. No bullying.
5. No inappropriate clothing. To be clear, underwear should be worn *under* your other clothes.
6. No yo-yos.

Anyone found breaking these rules will be contacted by Mr. Gruber, the dean of discipline. The punishment is swift and effective but very different from what rule breakers may have experienced in the past. According to eighth grader Jordan Rozelle, a frequent recipient of detention when she was at Horsemouth Middle School, Kaboom Academy's method is a welcome improvement.

"At Horsemouth Middle I was forced to write dumb sentences on the board over and over, which is really a waste of everybody's time and didn't change my behavior one bit. Writing 'I will not put gum in other people's hair' did not stop me from craving the amazing satisfaction of that particular thrill. But one session with Mr. Gruber and I've been cured for good."

Nobody knew exactly how the fight began, only how it ended: with the entire cafeteria floor covered in a thin layer of orange Jell-O.

"We were there . . . ," announced Aliya.

". . . and we saw the whole thing," Taliya finished firmly.

"I got pictures!" Leo added happily. "That is, I think I did. I pointed the camera in the direction of the shouting. I'm sure I got something."

"Excellent! Sounds like front-page news," Jory said. He didn't want the dodgeballs to be the lead story; that belonged on the sports page. And Victoria's article about the book pills was too sedate. Victoria would probably complain if her story had the smaller headline, but he would deal with that later.

"So what happened?" Ruben said.

Aliya sat on top of the table and crossed her legs. "Well, the fight was between Cole Butkovitch, Marlon Snipe, and Janno Crow."

"They each wanted the last plate of chicken nuggets," Taliya continued, joining her sister on top of the table.

Leo gave a low whistle. "No wonder there was a fight if those three were clumped together in line. Marlon has a hot temper, Cole is stubborn, and Janno is just plain mean, even meaner than Victoria."

"I'm not mean, I'm just painfully honest, you sightless mole," Victoria snapped.

"What's so great about chicken nuggets?" Margo said. She herself didn't care for any food that came in the form of a nugget.

"Nothing, except the other options that day were 'chicken-y nuggets' . . ."

". . . 'chicken-like nuggets' . . ."

". . . and 'tastes-like-chicken nuggets.' So if you were in the mood for chicken nuggets . . ."

". . . the best choice was the item actually called 'chicken nuggets.'"

"That's why there was only one plate left of the chicken nuggets . . ."

". . . and several plates left of the other options."

"Anyway, while they were fighting . . ."

". . . Cole threw a bowl of Jell-O at Marlon . . ."

". . . Marlon threw a bowl of Jell-O at Janno . . ."

". . . Janno threw a bowl of Jell-O at Cole . . ."

". . . and they kept throwing more and more Jell-O until the entire floor was covered with orange goo!"

"Where did all the Jell-O come from?" Victoria asked.

"Ah, I can explain zat, *mademoiselle,*" the musketeer said in a thick French accent, twisting the tip of his debonair mustache. "Today was what you call ze 'bottomless Jell-O bowl' day. If you bought a bowl of Jell-O, you could get as many free refills as you wanted. Ze cafeteria workers had no idea zat ze Jell-O was being used as projectiles, only zat zey needed to replace ze bowls as zey were taken. Voila!"

"Shut up, Sam," Victoria said.

"En garde!" said the musketeer, pointing his plastic saber at Victoria. She grabbed the blade and snapped off the tip.

"This sounds like a great story," Jory repeated. "Follow

up on it. Find out what happened to Cole, Janno, and Marlon." Aliya and Taliya grinned, both giving Jory a thumbs-up.

"Will do . . ."

". . . Chief!"

After school Aliya and Taliya noticed Mr. Gruber, the eighth-grade science teacher who doubled as the dean of discipline, leading the three culprits into his classroom. The twins looked at each other and nodded. That must be where Cole, Marlon, and Janno were going to serve out their punishment. The sisters would have to try to catch one of them tomorrow and interview him (or her) to find out what happened.

The next morning as the sisters got onto the bus, they spotted Marlon sitting ten rows back from the front. Usually he was loud and rowdy, but this morning he seemed very quiet, almost timid. The two girls sat in front of him.

"Hi, Marlon . . . ," Aliya said, leaning over the seat. He stared at the twins, his eyes darting nervously from one to the other. If Marlon hadn't been buckled in, the twins were pretty certain he would've jumped out the window. "How was detention?" Taliya asked. The girls waited for an answer, but Marlon remained silent.

"Was it horrible?" Aliya persisted. "Did Mr. Gruber hit you?"

"Did he give you mindless work to do?" asked Taliya.

"Did he call your parents?"

"Do you have to do more detention after school today?"

Marlon said not a word as his nose twitched nervously.

"Well, when you're in the mood to talk . . . ," Aliya began.

". . . we'd love to interview you . . . ," Taliya continued.

". . . to get your side . . ."

". . . of the story." The girls turned back around in their seat, sharing a concerned look. What happened to him? Why was he so jumpy? This story was bigger than they thought.

When the bus reached the school and the doors opened, Marlon was the first one off. Bolting from his seat, he scampered down the aisle, leaped out the door, and disappeared. Since he obviously wasn't interested in talking to them, the twins decided to try Cole, who had been sitting quietly in the back row.

The twins got off the bus and waited. They knew Cole would be the last one out, but after everyone was off the bus he still hadn't emerged. Aliya and Taliya poked their heads through the bus door to find him making his way down the aisle, trudging along carefully, practically moving in slow motion.

"What's taking you . . ."

". . . so long?" the twins said, exasperated.

Cole just looked at them and blinked. Then he did something unusual. He sat down on the floor and pulled his head into his sweater. He stayed that way for a full minute as the twins shared another concerned look. What was going on? What had happened to these students? Cole started to poke his head out, but as soon as he saw the twins still standing there, he drew it back in. Then the cannon sounded and Aliya and Taliya took off across the lawn. They ran through the double doors into the main

building, bypassing the lockers and slipping into the English classroom before the gong rang.

Several times during the day the girls tried to approach Marlon, but he darted away as soon as he saw them coming. Cole was easy to find, but he wasn't talking. He had parked himself in the courtyard with his head tucked into his sweater. Eventually he trudged down the hallway, stopping for a minute or two, then moving on to a different area, but always very, very slowly. Whenever anyone tried to talk to him, he retreated into his sweater. It wasn't until lunchtime, when the twins went into the bathroom to wash their hands, that they made some headway on their story.

"Hey! Aliya and Taliya! Is that you?" The voice seemed to be coming from the janitorial closet.

"Yes, it's us!" Aliya said, heading to the closet.

"Is that you, Janno?" asked Taliya.

"Yes! I'm locked in here! Get me out!"

The girls looked around for a key, but there wasn't one to be found.

"We can't find a key," Aliya said.

"We'll have to get the janitor," her sister said. "What are you doing . . ."

". . . in the closet, anyway?"

"I escaped and hid, but before I could get out, the janitor locked me in. I spent the night in here."

"Why did you hide?" asked Aliya.

"What's going on?" added Taliya.

"What happened to you guys . . ."

". . . during detention?"

"Just get me out," Janno said, "and I'll give you an exclusive."

• • •

It took ten minutes to find the janitor. Mr. Parker unlocked the closet, no questions asked, and then went back about his business.

"That's funny, you would think he'd wonder how I got locked in there," Janno said. Her shirt was still stained from the orange Jell-O, her hair was a mess, and she smelled slightly of cleaning chemicals, which might be expected from a person who'd spent the night in a janitorial closet. "He didn't even seem surprised."

Aliya rubbed her chin thoughtfully. "You know, I have a feeling that as a janitor of this school . . ."

". . . this isn't the strangest thing he's seen," Taliya concluded, also rubbing her chin thoughtfully. "You would think everyone would be looking for you . . ."

". . . once your mom called the school . . ."

". . . to report that you didn't . . ."

". . . come home on the late bus!"

Janno shook her head. "I called my mom from the closet and told her our science class was having an overnight stargazing retreat, and that I'd just forgotten to give her the permission slip, so I'd signed it for her. I didn't want her to find out about the detention."

"So then you also . . . ," Taliya started.

". . . signed the detention slip." Aliya finished.

"Good job, Sherlock Holmes," Janno said snidely to both of them.

"Well, that explains that," Taliya said, ignoring the comment. "Now tell us . . ."

". . . what happened." Aliya took out a small notepad and pen from the pencil case in her binder, and Taliya did the same. The twins waited, pens at the ready, eager for the story.

Janno glanced around nervously and motioned for the girls to follow her into one of the stalls. Closing the lid of the toilet, she took a seat while Aliya and Taliya squeezed in, shutting the door behind them.

"Yesterday after school, Cole, Marlon, and I met up with Mr. Gruber at his classroom. He told us to take a seat, which we did, and scolded us for being rowdy and making a mess with the Jell-O."

"So far this seems pretty standard," Aliya pointed out.

"No reason to be afraid," Taliya agreed.

"Hang on, I'm getting to it. And could you stop talking like that? I feel like I'm listening to a broken stereo."

"Sorry, we've been like this . . ."

". . . for as long as we can remember," the girls said.

"I was born first, and I always speak first . . . ," Aliya began.

". . . and I finish the thought," concluded Taliya.

"Well, it's weird and off-putting," said Janno. "Anyway, after the scolding, Mr. G. started talking about our behavior. He said that all three of us were too angry and tense, and that's why we are prone to fighting. He said we should relax, and that if we just calmed down, our behavior would improve. That's when it started getting weird. He went to his desk and brought out these huge eyeglasses. They had great big round lenses with a strange design that sort of swirled, but I didn't get a good look at them. He sat in front of Marlon, and . . ."

"Janno Crow! I know you're in here!" a voice called out, startling the girls.

Janno motioned for them to stand on the toilet so that their feet wouldn't be seen, but the ruckus they made trying to climb up there made it evident which stall they were in, and it was made even more obvious after Taliya lost her balance and clutched her sister, who in turn grabbed Janno, and the three of them tumbled through the stall door, landing in a heap.

Aliya and Taliya recognized Mr. Gruber immediately, for they had seen him walking through the campus during lunch. He had an oval head, a pear-shaped body, and two spindly, knock-kneed legs. Mr. Gruber looked like a big chicken.

"Ms. Crow, I believe you missed detention yesterday. That's unacceptable. You need to take responsibility for your actions. You'll have to serve your detention during lunch. Follow me, please."

Mr. Gruber crooked his finger at Janno, who stood there wide-eyed. She followed Mr. Gruber out the door, glancing back at the twins with a pleading expression, but of course there was nothing they could do. As soon as she left, the twins shared a knowing look. Without even speaking they had formulated a plan. If they were going to find out what happened during detention, one of them would have to *serve* detention. One of the twins would break a school rule and be subjected to whatever this mysterious punishment was. Immediately they both knew it would be Aliya. Taliya would remain on the outside, so to speak, and report on the situation. Because they could read each other's minds, Taliya would automatically know what her sister was experiencing. That was the theory, anyway.

The girls left the bathroom in silence, their minds a jumble of thoughts and emotions. They had never entertained the idea of separating like this before. The prospect of their doing two completely different things was disconcerting but also exciting.

There was a reason Aliya and Taliya Naji spoke in such a weird and offputting way, traveled together constantly, and did everything as though they were one person. It was because during the formative period of their lives, they were one person, sort of. Aliya and Taliya had been born conjoined twins, connected at the forehead, and they had in fact shared part of their brain. The operation to separate them was so difficult and the risk of causing brain damage so high, their parents decided to let the girls lead their lives connected. They did this for seven years. To Aliya and Taliya it was natural and normal. Of course their parents kept them hidden away from the rest of the world, fearing the negative attention the girls would get, the pictures of the "freak sisters" that would inevitably spread on the Internet. The Najis moved from Miami to a rural part of Florida, where they led a relatively happy life in seclusion. Mrs. Naji gave up her job as a teacher to homeschool the girls.

Then, only a few months after the girls turned seven, a group of brain surgeons from Harvard Medical School approached the Najis with a proposition. They had developed a new surgical technique that brought the risk factor for the two girls down considerably. The doctors had not had many opportunities to use it and needed the practice, so they made the Najis an incredible offer: they would do the surgery to separate Aliya and Taliya for free. The parents consulted the girls and everyone agreed that their quality of life would greatly improve if they were separated. The Najis gave the surgeons permission to operate. They moved the family to Boston to be close to the medical school; preparation for the surgery and the girls' recuperation afterward would take several months, and they wanted to be near the facility in case anything went wrong. After the whole ordeal was over and it was clear the operation had been a success, they moved farther north to Horsemouth, again seeking small-town isolation and privacy.

Once they were separated the girls remained close— perhaps too close. They knew they needed to make that final psychological step of behaving like two different people, but there was a great deal of comfort in having a sister who knew exactly what you were thinking and how you felt and who always agreed with you. So when Aliya and Taliya formulated this plan, in which they would each play different roles and have different responsibilities to carry out all on their own, it was a very big step.

The following day when they arrived at school, for the very first time Aliya and Taliya were not identical. Aliya had a yo-yo in her pocket. As soon as the girls got off the bus, Aliya removed it and started playing with it. Up and down, up and down, up and down it went. She was quite good at it. Taliya watched jealously, her fingers twitching to hold a yo-yo. She played with a rubber band that was in her pocket instead.

"Hey, Aliya, you're not allowed to have yo-yos in school," Jory said loudly. Jory, of course, had been filled in about the plan ahead of time. He was doing his part to draw attention to Aliya's degenerate behavior. "Aliya, I believe you are breaking a school rule!" he announced even more loudly.

"I don't care," Aliya said.

"It's a stupid rule," Taliya blurted. Aliya frowned at her sister. She wasn't supposed to say that. She was supposed to be the good twin, while Aliya was now supposed to be the evil twin. Taliya shrugged helplessly. The words had tumbled out of her mouth before she could stop them.

As they approached the entrance to the school, Mr. Gruber met them at the door. Aliya executed a very difficult trick called rock the cradle, which involved tossing out the yo-yo, grabbing the string to create a triangle, and rocking the yo-yo back and forth within it. She then released the whole apparatus, and the yo-yo spun smartly back into her palm. It was very impressive. Meanwhile,

Taliya knotted the rubber band around her fingers to keep them from moving. Inwardly she was quietly going crazy.

"Good morning, Aliya," Mr. Gruber said pleasantly. "Aliya Naji, right? Seventh grade? Perhaps you've forgotten, but yo-yos are against school rules."

"No, I didn't forget, Mr. Gruber," Aliya replied tartly.

"We just think the rule is stupid," Taliya mumbled, but she had shoved her fist into her mouth so that no one could hear her.

"What possible reason could there be for a ban on yo-yos?" Aliya said, with Taliya adding a quick "when they're just a toy" into her fist. Aliya executed an around the world, swinging the yo-yo in a wide circle. Suddenly the yo-yo flew off the string and hit Mr. Gruber square in the forehead. It hit his bald spot right in the center and immediately a circular red mark appeared, resembling a bulls-eye on a target.

"That's the reason," Mr. Gruber said, fighting the pain. "You may not believe this, but this is not the first time that has happened to me. Yo-yos hate me. I'm a yo-yo magnet. That's why when I was hired, I requested, *insisted,* we have the rule. It's in my contract."

"Oh. I'm sorry," Aliya said.

"If we'd known that, we wouldn't have done it," Taliya mumbled through a mouthful of fingers.

"Nevertheless, you've intentionally broken a rule. I'll see you at detention, three o'clock, room two-twelve." Mr. Gruber disappeared through the doors to go to the nurse's office for an ice pack, so he didn't see the twins' fist bump.

● ● ●

"I'm surprised that someone like you would be so reckless," Mr. Gruber said later that afternoon. "You really should act more like your sister."

Aliya sat in the front row of Mr. Gruber's classroom, nervously twisting her fingers. She needed to focus on what he was saying, but all she could think of was how badly she missed Taliya. She felt so lonely! She turned her attention back to Mr. Gruber and was surprised to see that he was now wearing the strange glasses that Janno had described. They had very thick opaque lenses, so she was unable to see his eyes, only a swirly rainbow of colors that was constantly shifting, and every once in a while sparkles would flash across them. They were quite pretty.

"Is this part of the punishment?" Aliya asked.

"It's not really a punishment. It's more like a therapy. It'll calm you down and give you a break from your rebellious attitude. We've found that taking a break allows students to realize that their behavior was all rather silly and unnecessary and that following the few rules we have is simply better for everyone. Now I need you to concentrate on something calm and soothing, something right here in the room that you can actually see . . . say, one of our lab animals. They're all pretty peaceful. Which one is your favorite?"

Aliya got up and inspected the small zoo in the back of the room. There was a rabbit, a guinea pig, a snake, a box turtle, a goldfish, and some mealworms.

"I guess I like the . . . ," Aliya started. She waited for Taliya to say the rest, but of course she didn't, because she wasn't in the room.

"I'm sorry, I didn't quite catch that. Did you say mealworms?"

"No! The mealworms are . . ." Aliya stopped again. Try as she might, the words wouldn't come. As she struggled to say "I like the goldfish," it dawned on her what had transpired with Cole, Marlon, and Janno. Now that she was standing right in front of the animal cages, it was all very clear. Hypnotherapy! That was it!

"I know what you're doing, you're hypnotizing students to behave like . . ."

". . . goldfish!" Taliya yelled quite out of the blue. The students in journalism class looked at her as though she were insane. Class had run several minutes late because they were learning to use the page layout program, and everyone wanted a turn manipulating the images on the screen. They were just gathering their backpacks when Taliya had her outburst.

"Are you all right?" asked Leo.

"I knew something was wrong when Tweedledum showed up without Tweedledee," Victoria said wryly.

". . . disgusting!" Taliya squeaked.

"Maybe someone should take Taliya to the nurse," Mr. Mister said.

". . . the animals they choose," Taliya blurted. She ran to the computer and started typing directly into the lay-out program, her fingers flying across the keyboard as she channeled the information from her sister.

"Wow, look at her go!" Ruben said.

Jory read the computer screen as Taliya typed, his eyes growing wider and wider.

". . . effects last for a day," Taliya murmured. "Marlon

chose the rabbit, Cole the turtle, and Janno the snake, which explains how at lunch today she ate an entire meatball sub without chewing. . . . Relaxing . . . wet . . . algae . . . treasure chest . . . bubbles . . . Oh my gosh!" she exclaimed, jumping to her feet. "It's done. It's really done. Aliya's been hypnotized into thinking she's a goldfish! Come on!"

Taliya bolted from the room, followed by the rest of her classmates. In no time they were at Mr. Gruber's science class, arriving just as Aliya emerged, wiggling her rear end and making kissing motions with her lips.

"Aliya? Are you okay?" Taliya moved toward her sister, who quickly wiggled down the hallway.

"How can she breathe on land?" murmured Margo as the group followed the elusive girl. They caught up with her at the end of the hall, where the janitor had left his cleaning cart momentarily. Taliya took a step toward Aliya, who darted behind the cart.

"Come on, Aliya," Taliya coaxed. "It's time to go home." But Aliya wouldn't budge. Taliya moved around to the other side of the cart, but Aliya slipped to the opposite side, always keeping the cart between them.

"Hey, you kids, stay away from my cleaning supplies," Mr. Parker said, returning from the janitorial closet with a mop.

"Sorry, we were just trying to get my sister to come with us," Taliya explained. "She thinks she's a fish. If we don't take her with us now, she could end up anywhere."

"She might end up flushed down the toilet!" Margo fretted.

"Why don't you just go fishing," Victoria said

sarcastically, but much to her surprise her suggestion was taken seriously.

"That's a good idea," Mr. Parker said. He cut a three-inch section of string from a ball of twine that he kept on the cart and handed it to Taliya. "Try this."

Taliya dangled the twine in front of Aliya's face as though it were a worm on a hook, instantly drawing Aliya's gaze. She wiggled eagerly toward her sister, who kept a gap of three feet between the two of them, and in this way Taliya led her twin down the hall and out the double doors, walking backward and jiggling the twine.

Twenty-four hours later, Aliya was back to being her old self except for one important thing: Aliya could start and finish her own sentences. So could Taliya. To celebrate, the next day they came to school wearing different-colored headbands. The yo-yo remained at home.

LEO'S STORY

Student Activist Stages Rally

By LEO REISS

So often kids are accused of being passive, preferring to watch TV, play video games, or spend hours on their computers rather than directly engage with their community. Not so at Kaboom Academy, where seventh grader Lee O'Reese led a group of over a hundred students in a rally to draw attention to the

needs of disabled students at the school. Though this reporter was part of the demonstration, he was unable to track down other participants for interviews. Indeed, with only fifty-five students enrolled in the school, it is a small mystery how so many demonstrators came to participate in the rally to begin with. That said, the event is one that will long be remembered.

Leo headed upstairs to Miss Schacher's classroom. It was only October and already he needed help with math. He wasn't surprised; this had happened every year for the past three years. Ever since he'd lost most of his vision the summer between fourth and fifth grades, he'd struggled to keep up in his classes. Leo was not much of a complainer—he didn't like to trouble other people with his problems—but even he had to admit that the last few years had been exceptionally rough.

A month after his tenth birthday, Leo started getting horrible headaches, accompanied by nausea and dizziness. He was thirsty all the time, and his vision was blurry. When his parents took him to the doctor, he was referred to a brain specialist, who put him through a series of tests, including a magnetic resonance imaging scan, or MRI, to take pictures of his brain. The procedure involved being stripped of anything metal that would be attracted to the magnets in the machine, lying on a slab with a thin blanket covering him up to his neck, and being fed into a tiny hole where he was told to remain perfectly still for close to an hour while being subjected to loud noises, all the while wondering if he was going to live or die. It did not help that his mother cried the entire time.

After getting the results the doctor diagnosed Leo with *craniopharyngioma,* a tumor near his pituitary gland at the base of his brain. The good news was that it was benign, meaning it was not cancerous, and that the prognosis for Leo's recovery was very good. The bad news was that once the doctors began the surgery to remove the tumor, they realized that the tumor had already done significant damage to Leo's optic nerve. Not only would his vision not improve, but it would most likely get worse.

It did get worse.

In one summer Leo went from being a popular Little League pitcher and skateboarder who had a good eye for drawing to a kid who would never be good at sports again, could barely see an object twenty feet ahead of himself, let alone draw it, and whose friends drifted away, uncomfortable with his condition. Leo could still see shapes and shadows, but sometimes he wished he had gone completely blind so he could don dark glasses, tap around with a white cane, use a Seeing Eye dog: the whole package. At least then people would believe he couldn't see anything. But without those physical manifestations of blindness, he only confused people. They kept forgetting about his condition, and once they were made aware it was too late— they had already passed judgment on him. He found out the hard way that first impressions really are important.

School became a nightmare. Leo could get around

his elementary school campus all right; after five years there—kindergarten through fourth—he knew the layout of the campus well. Even so, the school wasn't well equipped for somebody with limited vision. His parents didn't want Leo placed in a "special" class with kids who had learning disabilities, pointing out that "special" usually meant "remedial" and that Leo had been a very good student the previous year. Instead, Leo was mainstreamed with the rest of the student body, but of course he was not like the rest of the student body. He needed to press his nose up against a book to read it. He had to remind teachers to say out loud what they had written on the board because he couldn't see it, even from the front row. He made requests that the classroom not be rearranged or he wouldn't be able to find anything. He was forced to ask people to read the specials on the cafeteria menu for him. Nobody wanted to be paired with Leo because he was slower at getting assignments done. Every day he came home depressed, wanting to cry, angry, but as soon as he saw his mom, he sucked it all up.

As tough as the whole experience had been for him, it had been devastating to Leo's mother. She had gotten so worried and worked up, she'd stopped eating. It was weeks before she could look at Leo without bursting into tears. His mom still seemed so fragile; he didn't want to make it worse. He also felt guilty. Leo's parents couldn't have children; he had been adopted. For ten years he had been the perfect son to his father: joining him at ball games, helping him build stuff in the basement workroom, and sharing his father's obsession with airplanes to the point that they had planned for Leo to learn how to fly a plane before he was sixteen. He had also been a very good son to his mother. He could tell she got an immense amount of pleasure from having a healthy, handsome, helpful, and happy boy. But now he was damaged. He was not healthy and was far less helpful—in fact, *he* needed constant assistance. He couldn't tell if he was handsome—in the mirror his face was a blur. And he wasn't very happy; he was just hanging in there.

And what about his future? His plans to be a pilot had instantly evaporated. He thought the MRI machine was pretty cool, and he had gotten more interested in medical science recently, but what kind of job would he be able to get? It didn't matter how many times the doctor assured him that visually impaired people could live meaningful, active, and enriching lives; he didn't believe it, and neither did his parents. Sure, they *said* he'd be able to get a college degree, they *encouraged* him to aim high and dream big dreams, but meanwhile, his dad was making plans to remodel his basement work space into an apartment. Leo knew his parents were expecting him to live with them for the rest of his life. Nobody even mentioned the possibility of Leo meeting a girl and getting married. That idea landed firmly in the category of miracles.

Leo moaned out loud as he trudged up the second flight of stairs to the third floor. Thinking about his future gave him a stomachache. What if his parents adopted another child, a healthy one? He wouldn't blame them if they did. After all, who would care for them in their old age? Who would be able to support them when they truly needed it?

They probably wouldn't adopt again, though, out of consideration for his feelings. Thank goodness for that. Meanwhile, he would just try to make his problem appear to be as trivial as possible.

The only person who had made the experience bearable was Jory. Jory and Leo had long ago bonded over their interest in flying, Leo by plane, Jory by his own devices. They both liked to draw too. Leo sketched landscapes and imaginary worlds while Jory designed superheroes. After Leo's operation Jory came by to visit constantly, and even when it was clear that Leo's eyesight had been permanently damaged, Jory treated him the same as he always had. He never made Leo feel helpless or felt sorry for him. Somehow Jory knew that normality was what his friend wanted and needed most. At the same time Leo was struggling through his visual problems, Jory was dealing with his parents' separation and later, their divorce. In their mutual suffering the two were on a level playing field. They'd sit on Jory's roof, talking about flying and all the places they would go. Jory never once reminded Leo that he would probably never pilot a plane, and that if he did go anywhere interesting he wouldn't be able to see it. Leo really appreciated that.

Still, as much as Leo had Jory's support, and as much as he wanted to minimize the impact his blindness had on his life, the truth was that everything was harder for him, including the mundane aspects of school. Just navigating a new campus was hard, and now, walking down the hallway looking for Miss Schacher's room, Leo had to count the number of doors he passed, touching each one to figure out when he arrived at his destination, because he could not see the numbers over the classroom.

Leo knocked. "Come in!" a voice called out brightly. He opened the door and entered. From the smell of the room, he could tell Miss Schacher was eating her lunch—a tuna sandwich, if he wasn't mistaken. Being blind really did sharpen your other senses.

"Hello, Leo," Miss Schacher said. He could see her shadow rise from her desk and walk toward him. "I understand you're here for some tutoring."

"Yes, I didn't get a very good grade on the quiz," Leo admitted. "I thought I understood the material, but . . ." His voice trailed off as he held up his test paper. It had a red B− circled at the top. Miss Schacher took the quiz from him and looked it over.

"You know, it seems to me that you understand the concepts. There are just a lot of careless multiplication errors here." She handed the paper back. "Were you rushing?"

"Kind of. It takes me a little longer to read the problem because of, you know. . . ." Leo pointed at his glasses. He hated to admit that his poor vision was holding him back in any way. All of his teachers were supposed to have received a special notice about him so that he wouldn't have to keep explaining it. But if they had gotten such a notice, it was pretty apparent that most of his teachers either didn't believe it, didn't understand it, or didn't read it. Leo couldn't clearly see the expression on Miss Schacher's face, but her verbal response clued him in to the fact that she had no idea what he was talking about.

"I have no idea what you're talking about," Miss

Schacher said. "But listen. Over the years I've found that students who think they are bad at math aren't so much having trouble with the concepts as simply not grasping the basics. Have you ever used a multiplication table?"

"Yes, in third grade," Leo replied.

"So you know how to use it," she confirmed.

"Yes."

"Wonderful! I just got a new one. It's right over there." Leo glanced across the room in the direction where Miss Schacher was pointing, but all he could see were dark rectangular shadows on the wall. "Now I'm afraid there's a teacher's meeting in the auditorium during lunch that I can't miss, so I'll leave you with the multiplication table. Practice with it. Some people require that kind of visual aid."

Leo was going to tell her that visual aids were of little use to him, but she had already grabbed her sweater and was out the door. Leo sighed, heading to the back of the room. He walked right up to the wall until he was only a foot away and stared at the various posters. One was a picture of Albert Einstein. Next to it was a picture by M. C. Escher, a graphic artist who was a favorite of many mathematicians because of his depictions of impossible structures and the metamorphosis of images. Leo recognized this particular picture of an infinitely descending staircase from a book his family owned. The next poster was higher up and Leo was too short to see it. He stood on a table that was up against the wall so that he could get a closer look. As he climbed up there was a small flash of light, as though somebody had taken a picture, which of course he didn't notice.

The third poster was a humorous flow chart describing the process of a typical student's decision making when it came to studying. While reading the comments in the bubbles and chuckling, Leo heard a laugh right next to him. He was so surprised he nearly fell off the table. With him on the platform stood another person, and this person also had his nose only a few inches from the flow chart.

"Hey!" Leo said.

"Hi!" the boy said.

"What are you doing?"

"I'm reading this poster."

"I can see that. Are you making fun of me?" Leo said angrily.

"No. I have to look this closely. I can't see very well. I'm legally blind."

Leo blinked, surprised. He had no idea there was somebody else at the school with visual impairment. "You're kidding me. I'm legally blind too! What's your name?"

"Lee O'Reese. Seventh grade. I came in here to get some help with math, but the teacher took off."

"Yeah, I was here when that happened. I didn't know you were in the room, though."

"I came back here to look for the multiplication table, but I don't see it."

"Me either."

If the boys had knelt down and placed their noses an inch from the surface of the platform on which they were standing, they would have seen a small sign indicating that they were in fact on top of the multiplication table. The table to which Miss Schacher was referring was not a chart but an actual piece of furniture, and one of Dr.

Kaboom's many inventions. This is how it worked: a small dial on the side of the table could be set from one to twelve. Once it was set, any object placed on the table would be multiplied by that amount by pressing the button in the lower right-hand corner. If the dial was set for six and three pencils were placed on the surface, with the push of the button they would be instantly multiplied into eighteen pencils, all very real, all able to write, erase, break, and stick into the acoustic tiles in the ceiling if flicked just the right way. If the button was pushed again they would become 108 pencils. One more push would yield 648 pencils. It was a wonderful tool for people with good eyesight.

But it was not of much use to Leo, who had accidentally stepped on the button while climbing on top of the table. The dial had been set for two, so Leo had been instantly doubled. Unfortunately, when he hopped off the table, he accidentally brushed the dial, moving it to eight. Meanwhile, Lee sat on the edge of the table, swinging his feet.

"Nobody told me there was another kid here with the same issues I have," Leo said, excited.

"Me either," Lee said.

"I don't remember you from the first day. You sound familiar, though."

"So do you."

Leo was beside himself with happiness. As much as he liked Jory, here was a guy who totally understood all that he had been experiencing. As they talked it was clear that he and Lee had tons of things in common, from overly emotional moms to an interest in planes to not wanting to make a big deal about their impairment. Had Leo's eyesight been better, he would've seen that they had even more in common—their appearance, for instance. But all he could see of his new friend was a shadowy silhouette topped with a mass of blond hair. As they continued to discuss their mutual problems navigating school, Lee became agitated.

"When I thought it was just me, I was willing to put up with a lot, but there are two of us. Shouldn't this school try to accommodate us a little better?" Lee huffed. "Would it be so hard to print signs with bigger letters? Is it too much to ask for teachers to call on us by name so we know we're being addressed? How about putting some books with large print in the library? Would it kill them to provide the room numbers in Braille so we don't have to count the doors to figure out where we are?"

"I'm with you, buddy!" said Leo, pounding the table, inadvertently hitting the button. Instantly, seven copies of Lee appeared, making eight in all.

"I'm with you, buddy!" the seven new boys shouted from atop the table.

"Whoa! Where did all of you come from?" Leo gasped.

"We shouldn't have to hide our disability!" cried one boy.

"Yeah!" agreed another boy. "Why should we be ashamed of who we are?"

"We? Are all of you visually impaired too?" asked Leo.

With a resounding "yes" the boys began eagerly discussing their problems having to deal with people who didn't understand their condition, treated them like infants, ignored them, and refused to make the small gestures that would ease their difficulties. Leo counted the heads as best he could.

"I can't believe there are nine of us, we all have the same problems, and nobody has done anything about it!" Leo said, pounding the table and the button once more. Immediately sixty boys spilled off the table. Four remained on top, so that when Leo slammed the button one more time, shouting, "You know what? We don't have to take this anymore!" Twenty-eight more boys materialized and everyone tumbled off.

The room was now quite full of Leos, climbing over each other, wrestling one another, and getting into minor shoving matches as they scrambled to their feet. What the original Leo saw was a great, growing mountain of people who all understood him, supported him, and wanted significant change.

"What can we do?" Leo #7 asked.

"We need to demand that all aspects of the school be available to all students, even if they have a disability," Leo #59 answered.

"Most people would want to help if they knew the extent of our problems," Leo #26 added. "It's ignorance at work here, not malice."

"How do you educate people?" Leo #82 asked.

"What we need is a rally," the original Leo suggested. "We need to march onto the field. We need to make some noise and get people in the administration to take us seriously!" He tapped the shoulder of the gray blob to his right. "You, make up some flyers; just list bullet points of our grievances. Print it on something bright—neon yellow paper. A hundred will do." He tapped the shoulder of the gray blob to his left. "You, see if you can find a megaphone in the gym. I'm pretty sure Coach Freeman has one." He then addressed the gray blobs in front of him. "Ten of you guys go down to the art room. The teacher won't be there, everyone's at some kind of faculty meeting for the next hour. Look for poster board, long wooden dowels, paint, and pens. You're going to make posters. Two or three each should be good. Come up with a few simple slogans, nothing too complicated." Leo raised his voice so everyone could hear him. "Once everyone is done, meet the rest of us in the meadow by the cannon in half an hour."

"What'll the rest of us do?" Leo #2, also known as Lee O'Reese, asked.

"Come up with chants. While we chant, we'll march, all around the school, through each building, on every floor! Everyone's going to see us, and everyone's going to know we mean business!"

Leo had no idea that he was having this inspiring dialogue with himself, and that this new activism had been within him all along, he'd just been suppressing it. It felt good to express his anger and frustration. For the first time in years, he felt powerful. He felt so invigorated it didn't occur to him to question how so many boys suddenly appeared and how they now outnumbered the rest of the student body.

The various Leos left to carry out their assignments as the others stayed behind in Miss Schacher's classroom to come up with chants. Lee came up with the best one, a repeating chant to a military cadence:

I DON'T KNOW BUT I'VE BEEN TOLD
I don't know but I've been told
KABOOM ACADEMY'S REALLY COLD
Kaboom Academy's really cold.
THEY DON'T CARE THAT I CAN'T SEE
They don't care that I can't see,
I JUST WANT INDEPENDENCY
I just want independency!

Shouting as loudly as they could, Lee led the group through the hall, down the stairs, along the second-floor hall, down another flight, and past the classrooms on the first floor. Doors opened as teachers and students stared at the strange parade of blond, spectacled boys all wearing the same outfit, which en masse looked like a sort of uniform. The parade continued through the administration building, around the courtyard, and to the field, where the Leos gathered around the cannon. Newly made picket signs were passed around and raised:

I MAY BE BLIND, BUT EVEN I CAN SEE WE NEED CHANGE!

WE ARE BLIND, NOT INVISIBLE!

YOU HAVE SIGHT, NOW GAIN INSIGHT!

The cannon sounded, marking the end of the lunch period. It was the perfect beginning to the event. As the boys lifted Leo to the top of the cannon, he realized he was taking a risk; he was now cutting math class and causing a major disruption, and he would certainly have to suffer the consequences—probably detention and maybe even a call home to his parents. He didn't waver, however. This was too important. Standing up there in front of all those people shouting for him to speak was an incredible rush, but he looked around for Lee, who he felt was much more articulate. Unable to pick him out of the crowd, Leo realized he couldn't wait any longer. The energy was palpable. The time for action was now. Raising the megaphone, he began.

As Leo outlined the grievances of the legally blind students, the rest of the seventh graders watched from the window of Miss Schacher's classroom, not sure what to make of the demonstration. There was Leo, leading a huge rally made up of what appeared to be a hundred copies of himself. He railed against the administration, accusing them of thoughtlessness and entreating them to make a few very simple adjustments that would ease the day-to-day lives of this significantly disabled group. Cheering after each point that he made, the crowd of Leos supported Leo 100 percent.

As the seventh graders watched, they were struck by Leo's confidence and his leadership. Most of them had never given any thought to what it must be like to confront the challenges he faced. Most of them also felt a bit guilty, knowing they'd misjudged Leo, treating him like a lesser human being.

"Looks like Leo used the multiplication table," commented Miss Schacher. "I just wish he weren't missing class. He's going to have to make up the work." Of course, there was very little work being done in the school at that moment, because all the students and teachers were watching the rally from the windows, but she was only trying to make a point.

"Oooh, there's something in this classroom that makes copies of people?" Aliya began.

"That has some very interesting possibilities," Taliya said. The girls shared a knowing look.

"You two leave it alone," barked Miss Schacher. "It already takes too long for you to finish a thought. I can't imagine what would happen if there were more of you."

"There are about a hundred kids down there," Victoria remarked. "What happens tomorrow when they all get in the cafeteria line at lunchtime?"

"Oh, they're all going to disappear in about twenty minutes," Miss Schacher said, checking her watch. "Copies made by the multiplication table aren't permanent. That's to keep people from counterfeiting money. Or creating private armies, like that one," Miss Schacher said, nodding in Leo's direction.

"Who's going to tell him he's been talking to himself all afternoon?" Edie said. Everyone exchanged glances. Clearly, none of them wanted to burst Leo's bubble.

"You know, he really doesn't want to be treated like a baby," Jory said finally. "I'll tell him, but later. Let him enjoy it for a while."

The Leo brigade lasted long enough for Leo to finish his speech, take a picture for the *Daily Dynamite,* and high-five several of the boys before they disappeared, dissolving into the atmosphere. Before Leo could rejoin the class, Mr. Gruber accosted him to discuss the rules regarding disruptive behavior and staging demonstrations. He didn't give Leo detention, however. Instead, he told him that Dr. Kaboom had heard his message and wanted to assure Leo that any failure to address his blindness had been completely unintentional. He would do what he could to educate the teachers and modify the campus to alleviate Leo's difficulties.

When Leo joined his classmates in journalism at the end of the day, they all congratulated him on his successful rally. Mr. Mister suggested that somebody write an article about it, and they all elected Leo to do so, since he had been present at the event's inception. Leo did so happily, knowing that for perhaps the first time, his voice was being heard.

For the next few days Leo searched for his comrades, but he was unable to find them. He was particularly sorry that Lee O'Reese had disappeared; he'd thought they had really bonded at the rally. When Leo asked Mr. Gruber if he knew what had happened to the rallying students, Mr. Gruber made some vague reference to their mass expulsion, giving the excuse that during the demonstration they'd trampled the flowers. Even though he was the dean of discipline, Mr. Gruber was an old softy at heart and didn't want to diminish Leo's accomplishment by telling him the truth.

But Mr. Gruber needn't have worried. A few days later Jory filled Leo in on what had really happened, and they laughed about it. The truth didn't change anything; Leo still felt elated from the experience. After taking charge and speaking his mind, Leo realized that he more than anyone had been selling himself short. His blindness would make his life more difficult; that was a fact he needed to acknowledge, not avoid. But his condition was not insurmountable. There were things he could do, things he *would* do. Finally, Leo could see his way to a future.

LESSON 3: INTERVIEWS

PHOTO BY LEO REISS

"Those of you who have already turned in your stories should be looking at my notes and suggestions and rewriting them," Mr. Mister said. "Now, who isn't working on something? Margo?"

"I've got a pretty good lead," Margo said slyly. "You know the cafeteria food? 'Tastes-like-chicken nuggets'? 'Chicken-y nuggets'? 'Chicken-like nuggets'? I'm going to find out what those nuggets are really made of."

"Great! That's real investigative reporting! How about you, Sam?"

"Deedle-deedle-dee, I've constructed puzzles three!" said the garden gnome in Sam's seat, stroking the fluffy white beard that reached down to his belt buckle. "I will deliver them on a cabbage leaf!"

"Sounds good . . . except for the cabbage leaf. Use the computer. Jory?"

"I thought I was just supposed to monitor everyone else."

"You also have to write an editorial, to introduce our first issue."

"Oh. Okay. What should it be about?"

"Anything you like, but it should be insightful, honest, clever, and probing . . . just make it the best thing you've ever written."

"Uh, right," Jory said. He was wishing he wasn't the editor in chief. He'd thought he wouldn't have to write anything. Now he was being asked to be brilliant. His mind started drifting to the open window, through which he could feel the cool breeze. How wonderful it would be to leave all this behind and just soar out into the wide-open sky.

Jory's greatest wish was to fly. He thought about it constantly, to the point of distraction. His psychiatrist attributed his obsession to a desire to escape, mainly because Jory's desire to fly started around the time his parents got a divorce. It had been an ugly period in his life, filled with yelling, accusations, his older brother getting in the middle of it to mediate, and his three-year-old brother crying for attention. In the end, his mother had thrown his father's belongings into the front yard. Yes, he had definitely wanted to escape that. Around that time he'd started climbing onto his roof to get away from it all. But his parents' divorce had happened years ago, and now they were cordial with one another, even friendly, joking around when his dad came to pick him and his brothers up for the weekend. So Jory didn't think flying was about escape, at least not now.

Sometimes Jory had dreams in which he was flying. The sensation of this dream flight was so indescribably glorious he eagerly went to bed every night with the hope that his subconscious would send him soaring. They didn't happen often, but when they did, he zoomed over vast meadows, buzzing over trees and skimming tall grass. Or he lazily drifted over sparkling lakes, a warm breeze brushing his cheeks. Sometimes he poked through cool, misty clouds to glide through an achingly beautiful blue sky. Once Jory dreamt that he went so high, he found himself in outer space, flying among planets, moons, stars, and asteroids, heading toward the distant glow of rainbow-colored galaxies. That dream had been the best he'd ever had, but try as he might to replicate it, it had not repeated. Jory knew then that flight didn't mean escape. It meant freedom.

But Jory was just as happy to keep his real flying exploits closer to Earth. His first attempt was to jump off the roof of his house holding an umbrella. It didn't work very well. He sustained a fractured wrist and multiple scratches from a rosebush. But as he did more research, his parachutes and gliders increased in sophistication; the materials he used were more effective, the aerodynamic engineering more successful. But nothing worked as well as he'd hoped. The glider he'd created to jump off the school building at the end of last year had been a particularly painful flop. It started out well enough, but the roof of the school wasn't sufficiently high for him to catch a good wind. The breeze carried him directly to the flagpole, where he hung for a full hour before anyone was able to get him down. It had been very humiliating.

After that stunt, Jory had started his sessions with Dr. Cornpepper. During their meetings they didn't talk much about flying; instead, they chatted about Jory's feelings about his family and friends. They discussed anger, fear, resentment, and depression. In Jory's opinion, these meetings were pointless. Dr. Cornpepper seemed to be digging around for something that wasn't there. Jory often found his mind drifting as he gazed out Dr. Cornpepper's window, wishing he could just launch himself into the atmosphere.

• • •

"Edie, I don't believe you've turned anything in yet," Mr. Mister said, tapping the table.

"No, I haven't come up with any good ideas," Edie admitted. "I've been working really hard, but nothing has caught my interest." That part was a lie. It was true she had been working hard, but many things had caught her interest, just not things that could be published in a school newspaper. Edie had been busily doing what she did best: digging up dirt on other students. She'd written her discoveries in her notebook:

1. Victoria Zacarias cries all the time. Major crybaby. Smart but emotionally weak. Must try to make a recording!
2. Aliya and Taliya Naji used to be joined at the head for seven years. Must find picture of them stuck together. Try medical journal.
3. Jory sees a psychiatrist once a week to discuss his death-wish activities. It's not working.
4. Ruben secretly takes ballet classes—not quite the tough guy he sets himself up to be. Get picture of him in tights! Nutcracker ballet coming up . . . buy tix!
5. Sam, Margo, and Leo—painfully pitiful, no need for investigation.

Edie was very pleased with what she had uncovered. It had taken a lot of diligence, spying on students between classes, tailing people after school, typing their names into search engines and seeing what popped up, eavesdropping on cell phone conversations during the bus ride back and forth to Kaboom Academy. But she had gotten so involved in studying her classmates that she'd forgotten to find a story for the *Daily Dynamite*.

"You know what we could use?" Mr. Mister tapped his fingertips on the steep slope of his chinless neck. "A good interview."

"An interview?" Edie's heart sank right to her shoes. An interview sounded exceptionally boring. Asking questions, jotting down the answers, then typing it up? Where was the excitement? Where was the drama?

"That's a great idea," chimed in Jory, trying to take

his editor in chief job seriously. "You should interview Dr. Kaboom. After all, he created this place. He must have collected a lot of interesting statistics in developing this school."

Edie seriously doubted that. "Interesting" and "statistics" did not belong in the same sentence. She did not want to conduct this interview, but now that the ball was rolling, there seemed to be no stopping it. "I've never interviewed anybody before," Edie said, which was true. The idea of getting information about someone by directly asking him or her questions was hard to grasp. "I kind of feel weird about it. Maybe Sam can do it."

"Interviews are simple," Mr. Mister assured her. "Come up with a list of questions you want to ask. Start with the simple ones, then move on to the ones that are more difficult: personal questions, or questions that force your subject to reveal something he or she doesn't want to reveal."

"How do you get them to do that?" Leo asked. "What if they refuse to answer?"

"Yeah, or if you get too personal, they might answer by punching you in the face," added Ruben. Everyone forced hearty laughs, but Edie could easily picture that scenario actually happening.

"True, you should take into account who you are interviewing. For example, when talking to a violent felon, you might not want to grill him about his bed-wetting. But generally, once you've warmed up your subjects with simple questions and put them at ease, you've got them hooked. It's a strange psychological phenomenon, but they won't want to stop the flow of conversation. They may feel uncomfortable about your questions, but they'll answer if they trust you."

This sounded a little more interesting, thought Edie. If she understood Mr. Mister correctly, it was like setting a trap. She was the spider weaving a web, poised to catch the fly unaware. Yes, this interview thing might be fun after all.

"Now, don't get the idea that interviewing people is easy," Mr. Mister cautioned. "It's something you need to practice. A good interviewer has a pleasant demeanor without being too chummy. He or she groups his questions thematically, all leading up to the Big Question. He or she listens for the answer and doesn't speak until the subject is finished answering. Sometimes just being quiet will force the subject to reveal more information than they intended to, just to fill the awkward silence."

"Really?" Edie was definitely intrigued now. She didn't know information gathering could be so simple.

"Let's practice," Mr. Mister suggested. "Aliya and Taliya, why don't you give it a shot? Just sit in these two chairs." Mr. Mister set two chairs facing each other at the front of the class. "Aliya is the interviewer and Taliya is the subject."

The twins sat in the seats. Aliya picked up her notebook and a pencil.

"Good afternoon. What is—"

"Taliya Naji," Taliya answered.

"How—"

"Thirteen."

"What is—"

"History, but I like math too."

"What would—"

"Maybe a pediatrician, or an archaeologist. I can't decide."

"Did you—"

"You know I did!" Taliya burst out laughing, and then Aliya joined her. They went on until Mr. Mister waved them away.

"Well, most interviews don't work quite so swiftly, or mysteriously. Let's try another pair. Victoria and Ruben. Ruben, you're the interviewer; Victoria, you're the subject."

Ruben and Victoria took their places. Ruben crossed his legs, and Victoria looked at him with the same consideration she might give a worm she'd found drying on hot pavement. Most kids were afraid of Ruben, but she wasn't like most kids.

"Thank you for meeting with me, Miss Zacarias," Ruben began. "Tell me, what is your favorite color?"

"Bloodred," Victoria answered. Ruben wrote down her response.

"Why are you so mean?"

"I'm not mean, I'm honest." Ruben jotted this down.

"What is fifteen percent of a hundred and sixty?"

"Twenty-four."

"And what is the unit rate if someone sold thirty apples over three hours?"

"Ten apples an hour." Ruben scribbled again in his notebook.

"Deedle-deedle-doria, I think Ruben is getting homework done by Victoria!" the garden gnome commented.

"I think you're right, Sam," Mr. Mister said. "Okay, out of the chairs, you two."

"Wait! I have one more question," Ruben said. "What is negative three-fifths divided by four-sevenths?"

"This interview is over," Victoria growled.

Mr. Mister sighed. "This isn't rocket science, folks. Let's do this right. I'll be the subject, and Edie, you be the interviewer. After all, you're the one who's going to have to speak with Dr. Kaboom. Now, I'm not going to take it easy on you. You need to be quick on your feet. An interview is a little like a mental boxing match, a test of wits, pitting one mind against another. So don't be surprised if when you jab me, I jab back. Got it?"

Edie nodded. "Got it."

"Start when you're ready." Mr. Mister folded his arms over his chest and leaned back, one leg crossed over the other, bouncing casually.

"Okay, well, what is your full name?"

"Mister Mister."

"I mean your first name as well as your last name."

"My first name is Mister."

"Really? Your name is Mr. Mister Mister?"

"Yes. I've answered the question, now move on."

"Sorry, it's just a strange kind of name."

"No stranger than Robert Roberts or William Williams. It's just a name." Mr. Mister Mister looked irritated. Edie moved on to another question.

"Okay, uh, how did you get this job?"

"What kind of question is that?" Moisture had started to collect on Mr. Mister's upper lip and a bead of sweat dripped from his forehead.

"I don't know, I can ask another one, I guess. . . ."

"No, forget it, I can answer this. Last spring I applied . . . I mean, I tried to apply but they wouldn't . . . that is, I submitted an application. . . ." Mr. Mister's hands trembled. His leg bounced more furiously than ever. "Stop looking at me like that! You're confusing me!"

"I'm sorry, I'm not trying to. It's a simple question. . . ."

"I . . . I can't . . . Stop badgering me!" Mr. Mister leaped to his feet, frantic. The students watched, stunned, as he paced the room, wild-eyed and agitated. "I said I applied, that's enough! Go on to your next question!"

"Well, ah, okay, what are your qualifications for teaching journalism? Have you ever worked at a newspaper?" Edie felt like she had pulled the pin from a grenade that would explode any second. She was not disappointed.

"Why are you persecuting me? Who put you up to this?" Mr. Mister screamed. "My probation officer? My social worker? My mother? Cat and mouse, cat and mouse, that's your little game, isn't it? But I'm not falling for it. Not this time. Not again! I used to live here before it became a school! I lived in room two ten! That was my safe place! *You're* the strangers. *You're* the ones who don't belong!"

And with that, Mr. Mister bolted from the room. The students waited a full minute before someone spoke.

"Deedle-deedle-doggin, methinks he's got butterflies

in his noggin," Sam the garden gnome said, wagging his finger.

Jory turned to Edie. "You think you're ready for your interview?"

Edie nodded. Dr. Kaboom definitely had some explaining to do.

EDIE'S STORY—PART ONE

PHOTO BY LEO REISS

New School on the Block

By EDIE EVERMINT

Kaboom Academy, possibly the most unusual private school in the country, and certainly the noisiest, uses fantastically offbeat teaching tools and techniques. Named after its founder, Dr. Marcel S. "Hot Mustard" Kaboom, the academy is situated on five acres of land twenty-two miles northwest

 of downtown Horsemouth. The school has twenty-five sixth graders, twenty seventh graders, and only ten brave eighth graders willing to take the chance that an experimental school can prepare them for high school.

Edie read over her introduction. It wasn't bad for a beginning, but she knew the meat of the story was her subject, Dr. Kaboom. She had already set up an appointment with his secretary to meet him for an interview at lunchtime the next day, but Edie had to make sure that she came in prepared. She had taken Mr. Mister's advice and written down her list of questions, putting the easy ones first and the more complex ones at the end. It was true that at first Edie had not been crazy about this assignment, but after formulating her questions, she found herself truly curious about the man who had created this school.

To come up with her list, Edie had started with a little research. First she'd done the obvious thing, which was to type Dr. Kaboom's name into the search engine on her computer. The names "Marcel S. Kaboom" and "Doctor Marcel S. Kaboom" yielded nothing. *Do you mean March Kabul?* the search engine asked. But when she clicked on that, it brought up sites promoting spring vacations in Afghanistan, so she was pretty sure she did not mean March Kabul.

Edie found it strange that a man who had founded a private academy would not have his accomplishments recorded somewhere on the Internet. But maybe she was just looking in the wrong place. She decided to search for information about Dr. Kaboom's areas of expertise, learnomology, thinkonomics, and edumechanics. Again she came up empty. *Did you mean dermatologist? Limnologist? Laryngologist?* queried the search engine. No she did not. *Did you mean theology? Theocracy?* Again, no. *Did you mean edu mechanics?* it asked, providing several sites with information about mechanical engineering. She didn't think so, but she clicked on a few just to confirm. She'd been right the first time. Her Internet research was a complete bust.

But it did help her formulate a list of questions. She wrote them down in her notebook.

QUESTIONS FOR DR. MARCEL S. KABOOM
1. Where were you born?
2. Where did you grow up?
3. Where did you go to college?
4. Are you married? Kids?
5. What are learnomology, thinkonomics, and edumechanics? Why does my computer not think these are real words?
6. Why did you create a junior high school?
7. What are your plans for the school?
8. How did you develop your teaching tools?
9. What's your real name? Who are you really?
10. What's your game?

Edie knew that she would have to ask those last two questions very carefully. After all, she was only thirteen years old. Dr. Kaboom was the head of the school, whereas she was only a student. She didn't want to appear rude or disrespectful; she might end up in Mr. Gruber's classroom, hypnotized into thinking she was a mealworm. Cole, Marlon, Janno, and Aliya seemed to have recovered from the hypnotherapy, but every once in a while she would catch Aliya making kissing motions with her lips, and Marlon had started keeping a carrot in his pocket. Edie definitely wanted to avoid being disciplined.

Perhaps she could ask the more dicey questions offhandedly, like she was just joking, then gauge his response. Would he laugh back and give a credible answer, or would he freak out like Mr. Mister? That was its own mystery! . . . But one thing at a time. "Be patient, Edie Evermint," she said to herself, as she often did. "Be persistent and observant and time will reveal all."

The next day after fourth period, Edie went to her locker and retrieved the list of questions to reread before the interview. Suddenly, a stampede of students charged through the hallway, screaming. She watched in amazement as they rushed by, and then she saw what had set them off: the four dodgeballs had returned, led by the abusive purple ball. They descended upon the students, terrorizing them, pounding them, nipping at them, caroming off the walls, banging into the lockers, and causing a great deal of confusion. The students fought them off, kicking and punching, but the balls returned with redoubled viciousness. Then they abruptly bounced off, escaping through the open door.

Ruben appeared at the end of the hallway, punching his fist into his open palm. "Where did they go?"

"They went that way," one of the kids said, pointing at the door.

"Thanks," Ruben said. He charged past Edie and was gone.

Edie shook her head. Things were getting very strange around here. She couldn't wait to hear Dr. Kaboom's explanation. Dr. Kaboom! The interview! She checked her watch. She had only two minutes to get to his office!

Edie shoved her notes into her binder and raced out the door, across the courtyard, and into the administration building. She bounded up the stairs, taking two at a time, finally arriving at Dr. Kaboom's office, out of breath and slightly sweaty.

"May I help you?" said a frumpy secretary with frizzy brown hair pinned into a messy bun. Edie glanced down at the desk, looking for the secretary's nameplate. It was a little hard to find, as the top of the desk was completely covered in clutter: numerous coffee cups, stacks of Post-its, piles of worn-down pencils, and a mound of paper clips. Finally she spied it: MRS. MARBLECOOK.

"Good afternoon, Mrs. Marblecook," Edie said pleasantly. "How are you today?" Edie knew that if you butter people up, they often become very free with information. Mrs. Marblecook probably knew a lot of things about Dr. Kaboom, so it wouldn't hurt to get on her good side.

"I'm well, thank you," Mrs. Marblecook said. "Is there something I can do for you, dear?"

"Yes, I'm from the school newspaper, the *Daily Dynamite*," Edie explained. "I'm here to interview Dr. Kaboom about his founding of the school."

"Oh my, that sounds wonderful."

"It will be wonderful," Edie assured her. "I'll be very quick. Is Dr. Kaboom free right now? I have an appointment."

"Oooh, I'm afraid that's not possible." Mrs. Marblecook offered a sympathetic look. "Dr. Kaboom is a very busy man. He had to step out for a moment. You'll have to make another appointment."

Rats. Edie knew sometimes these things happened when dealing with important people. Schedules can change at the last minute. "When is he available? Before or after school or during lunchtime works best for me."

"Okay, let's take a look at her schedule. . . ." Mrs. Marblecook consulted one of the several day calendars on her desk.

"*Her* schedule? I thought . . . Isn't Dr. Kaboom a man?"

"Yes, but I was talking about Mrs. Cookmarble, his secretary. She sits right next to me." Mrs. Marblecook gestured to a nearby desk that had a much tidier surface. The only things on it were a pencil holder with two freshly sharpened pencils in it, a stapler, a tape dispenser, and an appointment book, all neatly squared and precisely placed. There was also a nameplate that read MRS. COOKMARBLE. "Unfortunately, she's not here right now, and she's the one who makes Dr. Kaboom's appointments. I'm her assistant.

You'll have to make an appointment to come back later and speak with her."

"Can't you make his appointments while she's gone? The appointment book is just sitting on her desk."

"I'm sorry, dear, but setting up Dr. Kaboom's appointments is not in my job description. If you'd like, I can make an appointment for you to meet with Mrs. Cookmarble to make your appointment with Dr. Kaboom."

"Okay." Edie sighed. This seemed to be getting overly complicated, but she made an appointment with Mrs. Cookmarble for the next day, Thursday, at lunchtime. Meanwhile, she would try to do more research.

• • •

On Thursday, Edie showed up in the administrative office at her appointed time. Mrs. Marblecook was now sitting at Mrs. Cookmarble's spotless desk. There was more clutter on Mrs. Marblecook's desk than before. Now, in addition to all the desk supplies, there were several small spider plants, a large collection of family photos in various frames, a mass of thumbtacks, and a rubber-band ball the size of a honeydew melon.

"Good afternoon, Mrs. Marblecook," Edie said brightly. "I'm here for my appointment with Mrs. Cookmarble."

"I'm Mrs. Cookmarble," the woman snarled.

"Oh! Are you and Mrs. Marblecook identical twins?"

"Technically, yes. But only a nincompoop couldn't tell us apart." Edie looked at Mrs. Cookmarble closely. Mrs. Marblecook and Mrs. Cookmarble indeed had identical features, but their styles were completely opposite. Mrs. Marblecook's hair had been pinned in a messy bun, but Mrs. Cookmarble wore her hair in two tight braids wrapped around her head, with not a strand out of place. Mrs. Marblecook had worn a brightly patterned blouse and colorful, whimsical reading glasses, while Mrs. Cookmarble was dressed in a gray blouse buttoned all the way to the top, and her glasses had severe black frames.

"What? What is it?" Mrs. Cookmarble snapped. Edie realized she must have been staring.

"I'm sorry. I have an appointment with you to make an appointment with Dr. Kaboom."

"That responsibility now belongs to my assistant, Mrs. Marblecook," Mrs. Cookmarble said, hooking a thumb at Mrs. Marblecook's desk. "And she's out today."

"Can't you just fill in for her? The appointment book is right there on her desk." Edie pointed at the appointment book, which only yesterday had been on the desk she was now standing before.

"No, I've been training her for months, and I don't want to undermine her confidence by taking over at this very sensitive time," Mrs. Cookmarble said. "If you'd like, I can make an appointment for you to meet with Mrs. Marblecook to make an appointment with Dr. Kaboom, even though I am technically on my break for another four minutes."

Edie looked hard at Mrs. Cookmarble, who stared back smugly. Edie was pretty sure she was being given the runaround. "This is what comes with trying to get something done the straightforward way," she thought. But again, she didn't have much of a choice.

"Yes, please." Edie sighed.

She made the appointment for Friday morning, but she was through being nice. The next time she came back, she would be armed.

On Friday morning Edie didn't take the bus; she had her dad drive her to school on his way to work. Waving as he drove off, she checked the time on her cell phone. In half an hour the cannon and the gong would signal the start of classes. That was all the time she needed.

Edie had done an exceptional job researching her subject, if she did say so herself. She had gotten reams of information from newspaper articles, interviews with neighbors, and even a little good old-fashioned snooping. The night before, after her parents had gone to sleep, she had slipped out her bedroom window and ridden her bicycle to a small blue house with a broken picket fence. This was her subject's residence. She pushed open the front door, which had been left unlocked, to find some firsthand evidence. Yes, it was breaking and entering, but she didn't worry too much about being caught—her subject no longer lived there. Nobody did. But it wasn't Dr. Kaboom she was investigating. This time she had set her sights on somebody else. What she found in that house was shocking, and perfect for her purposes.

"Good morning, Mrs. Marblecook," Edie said sweetly. Mrs. Marblecook was sitting at her desk, practically hidden by the ever-growing pile of stuff that had gathered there. Edie noted that she now had several electric pencil sharpeners and a collection of scissors: twelve pairs, to be exact.

"Good morning, dear," Mrs. Marblecook replied. "I understand you met my sister yesterday, Mrs. Cookmarble."

"As a matter of fact, I did," Edie said. "She made an appointment for me to meet with you to make an appointment with Dr. Kaboom. So here I am, right on time."

"Yes, yes. Unfortunately, I'm going to have to cancel that appointment."

"Really." Edie crossed her arms, her patience wearing thin.

"Yes, I've had an accident." Mrs. Marblecook held up her hand. Her thumb was wrapped in gauze. "I've stubbed my thumb."

"I'm sorry to hear that."

"It makes it very painful for me to hold a pen."

"That's awful."

"It is awful. Tragic, even. I'm going to have a temporary secretary come in next week to take over my writing duties. You'll have to come back Monday."

"Maybe you can try writing with your left hand," Edie suggested, but the idea was met with sorrowful head shaking.

"Oh, if only! But my left hand has palsy." Mrs. Marblecook lifted her left hand, which wobbled and shook in a most exaggerated manner.

"That's interesting—it wasn't shaking like that until just after you mentioned it," Edie pointed out.

"It only shakes when I'm thinking of writing something," Mrs. Marblecook explained.

Edie was done pussyfooting around. "All right, Mrs. Marblecook—Mrs. Marianne Marblecook of sixteen-oh-three Cherry Tree Lane—I want to see Dr. Kaboom, and I want to see him as soon as possible. So open that appointment book, *please,* and make my appointment."

"How . . . how do you know where I live?"

"I know a lot about you, and if you don't do as I ask, *please,* I will let everybody know what I know. You'll be ruined. You'll be fired. Anyone who knows you will mock you—that is, if they don't run you out of town."

"You're bluffing," Mrs. Marblecook said warily.

"I'm not bluffing," Edie said. "You, Mrs. Marblecook, Mrs. Marianne Marblecook of sixteen-oh-three Cherry Tree Lane, are a hoarder."

"Why, I never!"

"Oh yes, you are. I looked you up on the Internet. It wasn't hard. You're such an extreme case there is tons of information about you. You've been documented in *Psychology Weekly;* that's where I got most of your story, though twelve years ago there were plenty of newspaper articles about you, before you . . . went away." Mrs. Marblecook chewed her lip nervously, eyes darting guiltily from side to side. She didn't deny the charge, so Edie continued, flaunting her impeccable research.

"You are obsessed with office supplies. Over the years you've collected tons, and by 'collected' I mean looted. You've stolen from every office you've worked at. I've been to your house and, whoa, is that a sight to see! Mountains of paper, pencils, pens, markers, notepads, paper clips, staplers, whiteboards, and corkboards! Forests of floor lamps! Oceans of coffeemakers and watercoolers! I don't know how you did it, but I counted at least fifty swivel chairs, twenty desks, and twelve copy machines, just stacked on top of one another."

Mrs. Marblecook squeezed her not-very-injured thumb

with her perfectly good left hand, tears streaming down her face. "It's true. It's true! I am a hoarder . . . and yes, a thief. And I'm not a twin, I only pretend to be so that I can take twice as many office supplies. But pity me! Because of my illness I lost all my friends!"

"I can't say I blame them," Edie scolded. "No one wants to hang around a pack rat."

"No, you don't understand. I literally lost them in all that clutter. One night Mary, Sandy, and Gloria came over to play bridge. But during the evening one lost her way to the bathroom, one lost her way to the kitchen, and one lost her way to the front door. They disappeared in that maze of tunnels and passageways through all my stuff. I searched for them, I could hear them calling, but I just couldn't find them! Eventually, Mary and Sandy dug their own tunnels to escape through the dog door. But Gloria . . . poor Gloria. She was reported missing. The police came in . . . and . . . and . . ." Mrs. Marblecook hung her head, unable to continue.

"You were committed to a psychiatric facility."

"Yes. It was a lovely place, though. My room was two rooms down from Mr. Mister's."

Edie startled. "What did you say?"

Mrs. Marblecook's mouth fell open as she realized she'd probably said too much. "Oh, you didn't know about that?"

"I didn't know about what?"

"I've got to go," Mrs. Marblecook said, rising quickly. She hastened down the hall but then turned abruptly, rushing back to her desk and scooping as many of the items as she could into her large purse, including two cups brimming with hot coffee. She gave Edie a tight smile and hurried away.

Edie wasn't sure what all this meant. Would Mrs. Marblecook return with Mr. Gruber? In making such a threat to a school employee, had she seriously over-stepped her boundaries? Probably. Was she going to get in big trouble? Most definitely. Well, she'd gotten in trouble before. At least she could meet Dr. Kaboom, conduct the interview, and write the story before she was expelled. If she could figure out the truth surrounding this bizarre school, it might actually be worth it.

Edie took a deep breath and approached Dr. Kaboom's office. She knocked on the door, right below a nameplate that read DR. MARCEL S. KABOOM—HEADMASTER. "Headmaster"? So that was what "Hot Mustard" meant! Edie listened for a response, but there was none. She knocked again. Nothing. She glanced around to see if anyone was watching her, but Mrs. Marblecook was nowhere to be seen.

Edie opened the door just a crack and put her mouth up to the opening. "Helloooo? Dr. Kaboom? Anybody in here?" she called. Like Goldilocks, she took the ensuing silence as an open invitation and let herself in, closing the door behind her.

Dr. Kaboom's office seemed stark. A desk was near the window, but it had nothing on it—no supplies, desk toys, family pictures, or coffee mugs; not even a computer. The only things on it were a dead fly and dust. In another part of the room sat a sofa and an armchair with the price tags still on them. The walls were blank save for a small evacuation-procedure map for fire or other disaster, and a fire extinguisher. No doctoral certificates or college diplomas. No fun artwork that might reveal his personality. Just blank. Even the plastic plant in the corner still had the price sticker on it, stuck to one of the dusty leaves.

There were two doors to the right of the desk. Edie opened the one on the left. It was a closet, containing two suits, one dark blue, the other tan. She remembered that Dr. Kaboom had worn the dark blue suit at the opening assembly. There were also two collared shirts, two ties, and two pairs of shoes. Why Dr. Kaboom needed two complete outfits in his closet she couldn't fathom. Did he arrive at school in his underwear? Quickly, she checked the pockets. The blue suit was clean, but in the tan suit she found several business cards for the Bravington Bijou, a beautiful old theater in nearby Bravington. She'd been there before to see a play—*The Jungle Book*. Pocketing the cards, adding theft to her list of school infractions, she proceeded to open the second door.

When Edie saw what was behind it, her eyes lit up. She felt like Aladdin stumbling on the Cave of Wonders. This was the file room. Gray metal file cabinets lined both walls, illuminated by harsh fluorescent lighting. Most people would greet this vision with a wide yawn, but not Edie. She knew that this room was Kaboom Academy's information center. Within these cabinets were files on every student, every teacher, and every school employee. She couldn't believe her luck. She'd struck oil!

Edie stuck her head outside the office door and glanced around again, knowing there was no one there, but still . . . what she was about to do was so awful, so repulsive, and so, so exciting she just couldn't stand it. She checked her watch. Already she was late to her first class, and there were only forty-five minutes before her next one started. That wouldn't be nearly enough time; she had a lot of reading to do. Breathlessly, Edie pulled out the top drawer of the first cabinet and plucked out the front file.

MARGO'S STORY

Spices of Life

By MARGO FASSBINDER

Most high school cafeterias are known for tasteless, overcooked food that students would never eat in a million years, or for unhealthy food that contributes to teenage obesity. But Kaboom Academy has the most delicious food many students have ever tasted. It's not just a lunch;

it's an experience. Sixth grader Aaron Butkovitch states, "After eating in the cafeteria, I have more energy, I feel smarter, and no matter what I've eaten, my breath is really fresh. It's like going to the gym, the library, and the dentist all in one."

Yes, the food is amazing, yet some of these meals have suspiciously vague names: Meat-ish loaf. Tastes-like-chicken nuggets. Fishy sticks. Hamlike burgery surprise. What's the deal? What precisely are we eating? I decided to find out what's going on behind the kitchen doors.

The day before Edie confronted Mrs. Marblecook and discovered the file room, Margo steeled herself for her own confrontation. She had prepared for this day all week, gathering the courage to confront Lunch Lady Lois about the strange menu options. Now here she was, only a few feet from the lunch counter. The period was over and she could see Lunch Lady Lois going through the day's receipts. Her black hair was still packed under the hairnet, though a few wisps had fallen out over her forehead. She was an imposing woman, tall and bony, with a long nose that had a weird growth on the side of it and a chin that reached out so far you might be able to hang an ornament from it if you were so inclined.

Of course, nobody would dare do such a thing. Lunch Lady Lois had a bit of a temper and would certainly not tolerate that kind of foolishness. She was often heard screeching at students to keep the lines straight and moving and to clean up after themselves once they were finished eating. She also had a strict rule about backpacks. Because of their bulkiness and people's tendency to trip over them, backpacks were not allowed in the cafeteria. If Lunch Lady Lois spied a backpack, she would march out from behind the counter, snatch it up, carry it to the door, and hurl it out into the courtyard. She was very strong and could chuck backpacks quite a distance. Students wondered if she had ever competed at the Olympics in discus throwing.

But Lunch Lady Lois's temper wasn't the only thing that held Margo back. She knew that the story she was writing had the potential for being big. Really big. It could open up an incredible scandal. Practically all the students ate the cafeteria food, and if it turned out that they were eating something improper, it would affect everybody. She knew that in investigating food quality, one ran the risk of uncovering something very unpleasant. In the 1900s a book called *The Jungle* by Upton Sinclair had described horrible conditions in meat-packing plants and drawn attention to the need to clean up that industry. And now . . . nobody wanted to know what hot dogs, sausage, Spam, head cheese, and blood pudding were really made of. She was certain that once she found out what was really in meat-ish loaf and tastes-like-chicken nuggets, she would get sick to her stomach. There was also a good chance she would become an avowed vegetarian. She didn't particularly like vegetables, but she knew it would probably happen just the same. It would be worth it.

Margo girded herself, clutching her voice-recording cell phone firmly as she approached the cash register, where Lunch Lady Lois was going through the receipts. She stood there for a full two minutes trying to figure out what to say.

Lunch Lady Lois spoke first. "You're blocking my light," she said, a strange comment since the room was illuminated by overhead fluorescent lights and Margo couldn't possibly be blocking them.

"I'm sorry," Margo mumbled. Then she remembered how important her story was and gained some confidence. "Good morning, Lunch Lady Lois. . . ."

"It's afternoon."

"Right you are. Good afternoon. My name is Margo Fassbinder, and I was wondering if I could interview you for the *Daily Dynamite,* our school newspaper."

"Really? What about?" Lunch Lady Lois stopped what she was doing and put her pencil down, regarding Margo through narrowed eyes.

Margo gulped. "Ma'am, I would like to know, what exactly are the ingredients that you put in the food? What are our meals made of? You should know that I am recording your answer." She started the recording application and held her phone forward, waiting for Lunch Lady Lois to explode. Instead, she frowned.

"I don't understand. Are you planning on following these recipes at home?"

"No, I just want a clear explanation as to why the menu options have suspicious names. For instance, exactly what kind of meat is in meat-ish loaf?"

"Oh, that's easy. My recipe calls for a mixture of ground beef and ground pork."

"And what else?" Margo said accusingly. "Sawdust? Horse hooves? Rat hair?"

"What a peculiar little girl you are," Lunch Lady Lois said, crossing her arms over her chest. "There are some seasoned bread crumbs, egg, chopped onion, and a little milk, if that's what you mean."

"If there's nothing odd in the mixture, then why do you call it meat-ish loaf instead of meat loaf?"

"Well, you can hardly argue that beef and pork aren't meat-ish."

"Yes I can. 'Meat-ish' implies that it is *like* meat, or that it *approximates* meat. Beef and pork are *actual* meat."

"Have you tried the meat-ish loaf? It's really good."

"What it tastes like is beside the point," Margo said, frustrated. Lunch Lady Lois was acting very cool. Margo had to find a way to break her. "What about tastes-like-chicken nuggets? What kind of meat is that?"

"It's chicken."

"Then why do you call it tastes-like-chicken?"

"Chicken does taste like chicken, doesn't it?"

"Well, yes," Margo had to admit. "But a lot of things that people wouldn't want to eat taste like chicken. Rats, for instance. And lizards."

"How do you know that?" Lunch Lady Lois asked.

"I'm not the one on trial here," Margo snapped.

"I wasn't aware that I was on trial either," Lunch Lady Lois said, her eyebrows raised. "Come with me. I want to show you something."

Lunch Lady Lois crooked a long knobby finger. Margo hesitated for a moment, then followed her into the kitchen. They passed the counters, the ovens, and the sinks, where

Manny, the kitchen attendant, was scrubbing pots and pans. They stopped in front of the freezer. "You want to know what I put in the food? I keep all the meat in here," Lunch Lady Lois said, opening the huge stainless steel freezer door. Immediately, a blast of cold air hit Margo and she shivered. "Go ahead. Go on in," Lunch Lady Lois prompted.

"Why, so you can lock me in there? I know you're up to something."

"My, how distrustful you are. I'll go in first. You can stand between me and the door."

Lunch Lady Lois walked into the freezer and waited while Margo checked the shelves. The freezer wasn't large, maybe twelve feet by fifteen feet. There were five levels of shelving, which were organized according to types of food: a variety of ground meats, bacon, beef, chicken, and fish, all clearly labeled. They looked clean and delicious, even though they were frozen. There was also a lot of ice cream.

"How do I know this is the only freezer?" Margo said.

"You can look around," Lunch Lady Lois said. "It's not that big a kitchen. Listen, I don't have time to play anymore. I need to make a shopping list." She gestured for Margo to exit the freezer, which she did. "Sorry I couldn't be more controversial," Lunch Lady Lois said, closing the freezer door behind her. She quickly left the kitchen to go back to her receipts.

Margo plunked herself down on a stool, hitting her head with her fist a few times. This was so typical! She'd gotten all excited about an idea and it turned out to be 100 percent wrong. There was no story here at all. Once again, the only thing she'd proved was that she was a big screwup.

Her unfortunate reputation had begun to form when she was a mere toddler. Margo was the third of five girls. She had always felt lost and overlooked among her sisters because each of them had distinguished themselves in some way, whereas Margo had not. Hilary, the oldest, was the math-science sister; then came Jeanne, the visual artist; then Margo, who liked to think of herself as "under construction." After Margo came Emma, the athlete, and then the youngest, Penny, who was the performer. Everyone had heard of the Fassbinder sisters because they had won many awards and appeared in the local newspaper on a fairly regular basis; all except Margo. That was because nobody hands out awards for clumsiness or muddle-headedness. Margo did appear in the newspaper once, however. After watching Emma execute an amazing yoga pose, Margo tried to copy her, hooking her right leg behind her head, and after that, her left leg. The problem was, she couldn't unhook them. Margo didn't realize that Emma was about a thousand times more limber than she was, and now she was stuck with her head between her legs in a granny knot. After half an hour of the four sisters trying to untangle Margo without breaking her legs, Hilary finally called the paramedics. Jeanne took a rather embarrassing photo of the incident that appeared in the *Horsemouth Hornblower* alongside an article with the headline "Local Girl Wrestles Self."

Because her sisters were so amazing, Margo's utter lack of ability in everything she attempted glared all the more harshly. She had hoped journalism would be her thing, the activity that set her apart from her four sisters, a pursuit in which she could excel. After all, none of her sisters had claimed the mantle of being the writer of the family, and since she did like to write, maybe this would be her slot. But if her failure to find a story was any indication, that position in her family would remain unfilled.

While Margo pounded herself in the head, Manny approached quietly. She had seen him many times before; he was the person who put out more food as the trays were emptied. Lunch Lady Lois was the chef and the person who ran the operation, and Lunch Lady Kim and Lunch Lady Abby were the two overworked servers, but Manny seemed to do everything else. His attention was making her self-conscious, so she ceased the punishment.

"Why are you doing that to yourself?" Manny asked.

"I always smack myself around whenever I get something really wrong," Margo explained. "To remind myself not to get my hopes up. It doesn't work, though," she added with a sigh.

"I overheard what you said to Lunch Lady Lois, about the food not being what it's supposed to be."

"Yeah. Pretty stupid, huh? I shouldn't be disappointed, though. It does taste delicious."

"There's a good reason for that," Manny said, lowering his voice. He glanced at Lunch Lady Lois, who was continuing to do paperwork. "She does add something to the food to make it taste the way it does. I probably shouldn't be telling you this, but I see a lot of things in this kitchen, a *lot*. And I don't want you to hit yourself in the head like that when you don't deserve it."

"You mean, there *is* something in the food?" Margo squeaked.

"Yes. A very special ingredient."

"What's that?" she whispered, her eyes wide. Margo's fingers trembled as she hit record on her phone app.

"The secret ingredient is . . . love."

"Oh, give me a break!" Margo snapped.

"Shhh!" Manny cautioned. Fortunately, Lunch Lady Lois was completely absorbed in her task and hadn't noticed the outburst.

"I'm sorry, but you got my hopes up and then you served me that baloney," Margo complained. "She makes her food with love. I mean, really? I've got to go. I need to find another story to mess up."

"But it's true," Manny insisted. He grabbed Margo's arm as she passed him. "You seem like a nice kid. You didn't mess this up. I'll show you."

Manny took one more glance at Lunch Lady Lois as he crossed to the stove. It was a huge black iron industrial appliance with eight burners and two ovens beneath it. On the counter next to it was a spice rack. "This is what she uses to season the food," Manny explained.

Margo read the labels. "Garlic powder, lemon pepper, onion salt, rosemary, thyme, basil, oregano . . . so what? My mom uses these same spices."

Manny held up a finger and put his hand on a large metal box on the counter next to the spice rack. "But this is what she uses to give it flavor," Manny said. He took a key from his key ring and unlocked the box. Lifting the lid, he revealed another spice rack, but these spices were in small jam jars or simply in plastic bags. The containers were hand-labeled in a spidery cursive. Sometimes there wasn't even a name, simply a symbol. Margo was only able to decipher a few of them: *curiosity, patience, confidence, generosity, honesty.*

"What are all these?" Margo murmured.

"The spices of life," Manny answered. He held up a jar full of pink powder. On the label was an image of a heart with an arrow through it. "This is love, by the way," he said, handing it to Margo. She turned it over in her hand, holding it up to the light and peering at the contents. Diamondlike crystals glittered from within the pink dust.

"It's beautiful," she said, handing it back. "What's this one?" She pointed to a jar filled with what looked like sticky blue burrs, prickly and sharp, like something one might find matted in the fur of long-haired dogs.

"That's truth. It's hard to swallow."

"No offense, but these seem an awful lot like . . . well, like magic. Is Lunch Lady Lois a . . . a witch?"

"Isn't it obvious?" Manny gestured at Lunch Lady Lois, who had let her hair out of the netting. It snaked down her back in thick, luscious black coils. "Haven't you seen all the black cats roaming around the school grounds? Those are hers. She's crazy about black cats. That's her broom over there." Manny pointed to an ordinary-looking push broom standing in a corner.

"That doesn't look like a witch's broom. A witch's broom is supposed to be knobby and have a big clump of straw at the end."

"What era are you living in, the eighteenth century?" Manny laughed. "Witches don't ride those anymore. Do we still drive around in Model Ts?"

"But her teeth are so straight, and her hair isn't . . . you know, straggly."

"Last year she wore braces to fix her overbite. And anyone can find a good hair conditioner."

"Manny!" Lunch Lady Lois called from the counter. Manny quickly shut the spice rack while Margo ducked, which was unnecessary because you couldn't see the kitchen from the serving counter. Still, it seemed appropriate. "Manny, I need to know how we're doing on paper products. Do we need more napkins?"

"I'll be right there!" Manny called out. He turned to Margo. "You'd better leave. Go out the back way, into the alley."

"Can I write about this for the newspaper?"

"If you do, leave me out of it. I could lose my job."

"Thank you."

"You're welcome, and now you can stop hitting yourself in the head." Manny gave Margo a thumbs-up and pushed through the swinging door. She gave Manny a thumbs-up in return, even though he had already left the room. As she turned to leave, she noticed the key still in the metal box. She hesitated only a moment, then opened it and grabbed the jar with the heart on it. She poured about a quarter cup of the powder into a disposable glove she'd snatched from a box on the counter. She replaced the jar, closed and locked the spice rack lid, and tucked the glove into her pocket. The whole operation took less than fifteen seconds.

As Margo walked down the alley, whistling a tune, she felt wonderful, absolutely giddy. She had a story, but more important, Margo was going to spread a little love.

SNACK TIME

O n Friday, Margo arrived at the bus stop with a plate of chocolate chip cookies. Only the most discerning eye would be able to see the diamondlike crystals shimmering within the perfectly baked golden-brown treats. Margo was not that good a cook, but the powder had somehow rendered her cookies perfect. She had made them because she knew they were Victoria's favorite dessert. Margo had seen Victoria buy chocolate chip cookies at the cafeteria, three at a time. She planned to offer them

to her, savoring the moment when Victoria greedily gob-
bled them up, for the more cookies Victoria ate, the more
loving she would become.

That was the plan, anyway, but as soon as Margo got
on the bus, all hell broke loose.

"Hey, I smell cookies!" someone screamed. "Who has
cookies?"

"Oh my gosh, they're freshly baked!" yelled someone else.

"Margo has them!" cried the girl sitting next to Margo.
Margo couldn't hide the plate. It was sitting right on her
lap, covered with foil. Within seconds a small crowd
formed around her.

"Margo, is it your birthday?" "Did you make those?"
"Who are they for?" "Can I have one? Please? Pleeee-
aaaase!" they cried over one another.

"Sit down!" yelled Mr. Freeman, the bus driver who
doubled as the PE teacher. "Don't make me stop the bus!"

"You guys, you can't have any . . . ," Margo began, but
Aliya and Taliya interrupted her.

"That is so unfair," Taliya said, speaking first, which
she had begun to do recently.

"You're torturing us," agreed Aliya. "Those cookies
smell amazing!"

Margo realized then that the potion not only made the
cookies look irresistible, it made them smell irresistible too,
even though they had completely cooled . . . but no, wait.
The plate was still warm! These cookies were eternally
freshly baked! Margo guessed that if she buried these cookies in a time capsule and someone dug it up five hundred
years later, they would still be warm and smell delicious.

"But I made them for somebody." Margo could tell her plan was quickly falling apart. She would feel pretty stupid telling the whole bus she'd made cookies for Victoria.

"Who? A guy?" teased Ruben. "Leo? You made them for Leo? Or Jory?"

"No, not Leo or Jory," Margo said quickly. If she were going to make cookies for a guy, neither Leo nor Jory would be her first choice, though Jory was certainly exciting and Leo was very sweet. No, the only guy for whom she would make cookies was Sam. Sam was so quirky and mysterious. She wondered what he really looked like under all those costumes and wigs and makeup. He probably looked goofy, but in a cute sort of way. His eyes were the brightest blue, and his voice was so adorably husky. . . .

Margo should not have allowed her mind to wander. The next thing she knew, somebody had snatched the plate from her hands, and everyone on the bus was taking a cookie and passing the plate along to the next person.

"Stop!" Margo shouted desperately. "They're for Victoria! It's . . . it's her birthday!"

"It's not my birthday," Victoria said. "My birthday's in the summer, and you don't need to worry about getting me anything because if I do have a party, you won't be invited."

The plate had made its way up one side of the aisle, to the front of the bus. Even Mr. Freeman took a cookie and stuffed it into his mouth before sending the plate back down the other side of the aisle. Victoria now had the plate in her hands.

"Sorry, I must have been mistaken," Margo said. "Well, enjoy them anyway. I did make them for you. I know how much you like chocolate chip cookies."

"I don't like chocolate chip cookies," Victoria replied, passing the plate to the person behind her without taking one.

Margo's neck started to get hot. "But . . . I've seen you buy them at the cafeteria. . . ."

"The cafeteria makes chocolate *chunk* cookies. I absolutely love chocolate *chunk* cookies. I despise chocolate *chip* cookies."

"What's the difference?"

"Really? You don't know the difference between chocolate *chip* and chocolate *chunk*?"

"No!"

"One is *chunky,* while the other is *chippy,*" Victoria said drily, turning back to the book she had been reading. Meanwhile, everyone on the bus who had gotten a cookie eagerly munched away as the empty plate made its way back to Margo. She took the plate, balled her fingers into a tight little fist, and pounded herself in the head several times, against Manny's advice.

By third period, the powder in the cookies had started to take effect. As Margo expected, the love in the potion was not the romantic kind of love, but the love-of-your-fellow-man kind of love. Still, people were behaving in a way that could only be described as odd, and by seventh period "odd" had progressed to "disturbing."

For instance, in life science Margo was teamed up with Ruben to do a lab that involved looking at leaf and skin cells through a microscope. Normally, Margo did not enjoy being around Ruben. After Victoria, he was the meanest person in the class, at least to her. But she had seen him swallow a cookie in one bite and was curious to find out if it changed his behavior. Would he listen to her? Would he resist the urge to tease her when she got an answer wrong? Would he defend her if Victoria made fun of her? She was actually looking forward to this. What she got was a shock.

"We're supposed to look at the leaf cells first," Margo said, scooting her stool closer to the counter. The slides were in a box next to the microscope that they were going to share. She put the leaf cells into the slide holder. "Do you want to go first? I'll write down your observations."

"Why would you ask that? Are you implying I don't know how to write?" Ruben pouted.

"I didn't mean anything by it. . . ."

"I'm not stupid. I can write, you know. Just because I'm big people always think I'm dumb. I'm not dumb!"

"I'm sorry, Ruben, I didn't—"

"Well, you should think before you say something so hurtful."

Margo frowned. "Uh, okay, I'll look first and you write my observations."

"I can't believe you said that!" Ruben wailed.

"What?"

"What am I, your servant? Who died and left you in charge?"

"Well, how do you want to do it?" Margo said, frustrated.

"I can hear the sarcasm loud and clear," Ruben insisted. "You don't think I can come up with a plan. You think I'm an idiot."

Margo didn't want to respond. Everything she said only made it worse. She glanced around the classroom and realized nobody was getting anything done. Instead of looking at the slides, people were picking fights. This was definitely not a lovefest. Even Aliya and Taliya were at each other's throats. The only person in the room who wasn't arguing or crying was Victoria. She was doing the lab by herself, since Jory, her lab partner, was sitting on the ledge outside the window. Mr. Nash, the seventh-grade science teacher, called in Mr. Gruber, who arrived wearing the hypnotherapy glasses. Margo knew something had gone horribly wrong. Since nobody was paying much attention to her, she left.

She was glad to see that the cafeteria was open. She went inside and found Manny filling napkin dispensers.

"Hello, Manny," Margo said.

"Hello, Margo," Manny answered. "Lunch is over."

"I'm not here for lunch. I came to see you. I . . . I'm trying to write this article, and I have a few questions."

"Off the record?"

"Of course. Off the record."

"Okay, go ahead. Shoot."

"Well, how exactly does Lunch Lady Lois use those spices? Does she just dump one into a dish? Does she use a couple at a time?"

"Oh no! She doesn't dump anything. She takes one crystal at a time, very delicately, with a tweezer."

"A tweezer?"

"Of course. She doesn't want to use too much. That would be a disaster!"

"Huh. Really? A disaster, you say?"

"A colossal catastrophe! You know how they say you can't have too much of a good thing? That's not true. You *can* have too much of a good thing. Too much of these spices can be lethal! Think about it. People who are so honest they say something stupid that gets them killed. People so generous they give away everything, including what they need to live. People so curious they . . . well, you know curiosity killed the cat. It'll hurt people too if they're not careful."

"Oh my gosh. That's horrible!"

"No need to worry, Lunch Lady Lois knows what she is doing. She's very careful."

"That's very reassuring, but if someone did happen to overdose . . ."

"But that would never happen."

"I know, I know. Lunch Lady Lois is careful. . . ."

"*Very* careful."

"Okay! I get it! But if by some crazy set of circumstances somebody took too much of a spice, say the love spice, you know, the one with the heart symbol with a tear next to it, what would happen?"

"I couldn't begin to imagine. It just wouldn't happen in a million years."

Margo quickly realized Manny had outlasted his usefulness. "Well, thank you for your help," she said, making a beeline for the door.

"By the way, the love spice is in the jar with the heart that has an arrow through it. The heart with a tear is something else altogether."

Margo halted. "What did you say?"

"I just want to be sure you've got your facts straight for your story."

"Yes, of course. So what's the spice in the jar with the heart and the tear?"

"Sensitivity."

"Ah. Sensitivity. So I didn't even pick the right jar," Margo muttered woefully to herself. She made a fist and was just about to hit her head a few times, when an idea suddenly came to her and she bolted out the doors instead.

"That was all off the record!" Manny called after her as she sprinted across the courtyard, back to the academic building.

• • •

Nobody in the classroom had noticed Margo's disappearance; they were still in the throes of emotional turmoil. She had only one idea. She didn't like the idea, but she was responsible for this mess, so she knew she had to put her personal feelings aside if she was going to fix it. Only of course *she* couldn't fix it; she couldn't fix anything. All she did was get things wrong. But there was one person who could.

"Victoria, I need your help," Margo said. Victoria looked up from her microscope. Despite the chaos around her, Victoria had continued to do the assignment. After all, she still wanted to get a good grade.

"I was wondering when you were going to come over here. I knew you had to have something to do with all this." Victoria swept her hand across the scene. Even though Mr. Gruber had managed to get a few kids to start behaving like mealworms, the pandemonium had not significantly reduced.

"What makes you think I had anything to do with it?"

"You're the only other kid who's not acting crazy. And you tried to ply me with cookies this morning. There was something in them, wasn't there?"

Victoria certainly was smart. Margo had picked the right person. She admitted what she had done, from her botched story about the cafeteria food to finding out about the spices to stealing a sample to making the cookies . . . all the way up to when they had been passed around on the bus. During Margo's recitation Victoria's expression changed from disdain to disbelief and finally to something that was entirely unlikely: awe and wonder.

"So let me get this straight," Victoria said after Margo was finished. "You were so angry with me that not only did you steal something from the kitchen, but you tried to poison me and ended up poisoning everyone on the bus instead?"

Margo hung her head. It sounded pretty awful when put that way.

"Why, you evil little thing!" Victoria squealed. Margo couldn't believe her ears. Victoria wasn't mad; she was delighted. "I didn't know you had it in you!"

"You mean to mess things up on such a large scale?"

"No, to stand up for yourself. Good for you. But you're right. This is a monumental screwup. What do you expect me to do about it?"

Margo surveyed the classroom. Chairs were flying. People were screaming, shouting, poking each other in the chest, or just curled up crying and blubbering, their feelings so bruised they couldn't function. "Somebody could get hurt in all this," Margo said. "I mean, it's awful!"

"I think it's kind of funny."

Margo shook her head. "No, it's not. You do realize Jory is out on the ledge again. Besides, think of it as a challenge. I bet you're smart enough to figure out a way to stop it. It is just chemistry, after all."

Victoria knew she was being manipulated. Margo was appealing to her inflated ego, but the fact that she recognized the ploy didn't mean it wasn't effective. She went for it. "Take me to the kitchen," she ordered.

When the two girls entered the cafeteria, Lunch Lady Kim was getting ready to leave and was putting on her coat, while Lunch Lady Abby stood behind the cash register. Even though few students came in after lunch, it was the cafeteria's policy that the doors remained open until school let out, just in case a teacher or other school employee wanted to purchase something during his or her break. Lunch Lady Abby stifled a yawn, trying to keep her eyes open. It looked like she had put in a long day.

"You going to buy something?" Lunch Lady Abby said dully as the two girls approached the counter.

"No, thank you," Margo and Victoria said. Lunch Lady Abby shrugged and closed her eyes to let them rest, just for a minute.

Through the window in the kitchen door, the girls could see Lunch Lady Lois talking with Manny. After a few minutes Manny came out. He looked at Margo as if to say, "I don't know why you're here, but don't get me fired." Margo returned the look with one of her own, which assured him that she wouldn't. As Manny went about his business, Margo craned her neck to catch a glimpse through the still-swinging door.

"Look!" Margo whispered. "The spice box is open!"

"You've got to get Lunch Lady Lois out of the kitchen," Victoria said. "Then leave the rest to me."

"Me? How am I supposed to do that without messing it up?" Margo said.

"Margo, as much as it pains me to say this, you're not actually stupid, you're just impulsive. Think of a solution to the problem. Then, *before you do it,* think of what's wrong with it. Come up with a second idea, then think of what's wrong with *that* one. Then, if you light upon a third idea, hopefully that one will work."

Margo couldn't believe her ears. Was Victoria actually offering some encouraging remarks? Impossible. "Are you sure you didn't eat one of those cookies?" Margo probed.

"Of course not. I already told you. . . ." Victoria's eyes widened. "You know, when I was passing the plate, a couple of crumbs fell on my book. I believe I did pick them up and pop them into my mouth."

"That explains why you're helping me." Margo nodded. "And why you just gave me some good advice, without a sneer or any hint of sarcasm. You're a tiny bit sensitive to my predicament."

"What have you done to me?" Victoria cried, clutching her throat. "You've ruined me!"

"I'm really sorry. I'm sure it will wear off," Margo said. Meanwhile, she had already come up with her first idea: to set off the fire alarm. She thought about the drawbacks. True, it would get Lunch Lady Lois out of the kitchen, but everyone would have to vacate the building, including Victoria and her. Then they wouldn't be able to sneak in through the back door because somebody would be stationed there—it was part of the fire-safety procedures. So that wouldn't work. Instantly, she thought of a second idea. She would go into the kitchen and juggle some pots, then "accidentally" bonk Lunch Lady Lois on the head with a saucepan, knocking her out cold. Well, there were numerous things wrong with that idea, which she ticked off in her head:

1. Could cause serious injury.
2. No good reason why I would be juggling pots.
3. Can't juggle pots.

This wasn't good; the second idea was worse than the first. At this rate . . . But then a notion came to her. She thought about it. She thought about it again. She took the idea apart bit by bit. No matter how she rolled it over in her mind, it seemed sound. She turned to Victoria, who was worriedly scraping her tongue with her fingernails.

"I've got it. Follow me." Victoria stopped scraping and followed Margo into the kitchen, passing the snoozing Lunch Lady Abby.

The two girls approached Lunch Lady Lois as she came out of the freezer. Margo cleared her throat and Lunch Lady Lois turned around, surprised and slightly irritated. "Hello, Margo," she said. "You do realize you're not allowed back here? Besides, I thought you dropped that news story."

"Yes, I did, but I need to tell you something important."

"It'll have to wait. I'm very busy."

"I know, but—"

"Go on, get out. Come back tomorrow."

"But Lunch Lady Lois! *There's a black cat stuck on the roof!*"

Victoria rolled her eyes. Obviously, Margo should've come up with a fourth idea. But then Victoria saw Lunch

Lady Lois's irritated scowl soften, quickly melting to an expression of great concern.

"A black cat? Stuck on the roof? Why didn't you say so?"

"I tried! I heard him mewing, and then when I went to investigate, I saw that it was just a little black kitten. He looked so scared. I couldn't find the janitor, but—"

"We're wasting time," Lunch Lady Lois interrupted. "Poor thing! Where did you say he was?"

"Waaaay over on the auditorium roof," Margo said.

Lunch Lady Lois grabbed her broom and raced out the back door. Victoria turned to Margo, confused.

"She's a witch," Margo explained. "She has a soft spot for black cats. Quick, let's look at the spices."

The girls raced over to the special spice rack, which was still open. Victoria peered at the various labels.

"Let me see, what would be the best antidote for sensitivity? I assume there isn't a powder in here labeled 'insensitivity.' That would be too easy."

"I believe the spice rack contains only spices with positive attributes," Margo said. "Manny called them the spices of life."

Victoria continued to peruse the bags and jars. "Okay, maybe a jolt of confidence, mixed with some patience, some poise . . . This is hard. I really don't know if this will work."

"You can do it. I've got faith in you."

Victoria took the three powders and mixed them together in a small plastic bag, shaking it up and down. She peered at the mixture, which was a dull graphite gray. "Well? What do you think? Will it make people sick?"

"I don't know," Margo said hesitantly. "Something about it doesn't look right."

Victoria knew there was something wrong. She wasn't sure what it should look like, but this looked bad, like ashes. It smelled bad too, and her eyes started to sting. She could feel tears welling up. Rats! There was no place to run to, she thought, wiping her eyes with her sleeve.

"Are you okay?" Margo asked.

"Yeah. It's just hot in here. My eyes are sweating. Look, I have real reservations about giving this to anybody. I'm positive I screwed it up . . . I failed. . . ." At this point her voice caught in her throat and she wasn't able to continue.

Margo couldn't believe it. Those weren't sweat drops trickling from Victoria's eyes; they were tears! She hesitated, and then put her hand on Victoria's shaking shoulder. "Hey, Victoria! It's okay! It's okay to get something wrong once in a while, it won't kill you. If it did, I'd be dead a million times over. It just makes you human."

"No. I'm better than that."

"Better than human?"

"You don't understand." Victoria sighed. "I have to be right. Always. I have really high standards, and I always meet them. If I fall short, if I turn out ordinary like everyone else . . . I just . . . I'll disappoint everyone. I'll never forgive myself. Now listen to me. I'm going to eat this. I'm going to be the guinea pig."

"But what if it's poison?"

"That's fine. Then I won't have to live down my failure. By the way, if I die, don't give it to anyone else."

"I could have probably figured that out, but thanks for the heads-up."

After opening the bag, Victoria closed her eyes. As she did, Margo spotted a small vial on the far side of the rack. She had an idea. She thought about it, tried to come up with a second and third idea, but this first idea was a pretty good one. She opened the vial and shook some of its contents into the bag.

"Okay, go ahead," Margo said.

Victoria licked her fingertip, stuck it in the bag, and then delicately licked the mixture of powders off her finger. "Mmm." She opened her eyes, smiling. "Mmm! This is delicious!" She stuck her finger in the bag a second time, whirling it around to collect as much powder as possible, then popping it into her mouth and sucking her finger clean.

"It tastes like really sweet raspberry lemonade!"

"Yay!" Margo cried, clapping her hands. Victoria had her finger back in the bag. "Victoria, don't eat it all!" Margo chided. "We need to save it for the crazy, out-of-control mob!"

"Yeah, you're right. How are we going to get them to eat it?"

Margo came up with an idea. Then she got a second idea, and then a third idea. None of them were good. But her fourth idea . . . Her mouth spread into a wide grin. "Victoria, what's the one thing everyone at this school loves to eat? It's always got the longest line in the cafeteria."

"I'm with you." Victoria grinned back. "We are about to make some amazing smoothies!"

After the girls poured the spice mix into the smoothie machine, they were able to squeeze out thirty smoothies. They woke up Lunch Lady Abby and paid for them, then placed them on a cafeteria cart and wheeled them across the courtyard, where they passed Lunch Lady Lois coming back from her search, cradling a small black kitten. Both girls shot each other a confused look but then shrugged. There were so many black cats roaming around, there were probably several on every roof of the school.

Once in the academic building, they could see that the mayhem had poured out of the science room and into the hall. Other teachers and students had joined in, trying to get things back to order, but nobody was listening.

"PEOPLE!" Victoria roared. "ATTENTION! PEOPLE!" Her voice rose above the racket. "WE HAVE FREE SMOOTHIES! COME AND GET 'EM!"

That did the trick. Though several people complained that by offering the smoothies for free, Victoria was implying that they couldn't afford them, and others complained that she was insinuating that they needed to eat more healthily, every person lined up to receive the treat, even the teachers and the students who hadn't eaten the chocolate chip cookies. Soon the arguing and fighting and crying were replaced by the happy slurping of people sucking smoothies through straws. Margo and Victoria stood, hands on hips, surveying their success.

"Come on," Victoria said. "We'd better return this cart."

As the girls headed back to the cafeteria, Margo glanced at Victoria out of the corner of her eye. She looked relaxed and easygoing, and much prettier too. "Hey, so you succeeded after all," she said. "Thanks."

Victoria shook her head with a crooked smile. "No, I didn't."

"Of course you did."

"That mixture wasn't all mine. I heard you shake something into it at the last second. What was it?"

"Um, well, it was forgiveness."

"Ah. Makes perfect sense. So that once it was over, everyone would forgive you. Good thinking."

"Actually, I put it in there for you." Victoria slowed her stroll, turning to Margo questioningly. "So that if your mixture didn't work, you would forgive yourself," Margo explained.

Victoria stopped pushing the cart, folding her arms over her chest. "Why?"

"What do you mean, 'why'?"

"Why did you want to help me when I've only been mean to you? You could've blackmailed me, humiliated me . . . that's what I would've done."

Margo opened her mouth to respond, then stopped to think. "I don't know. One more thing I screwed up, I guess. Anyway, don't worry. It will probably wear off."

"I hope not," said Victoria, smiling, as she started to push the cart again. "You're pretty smart, you know that?"

Now it was Margo's turn to smile.

• • •

After Margo and Victoria returned the cart and began making their way back to the academic building, they saw Edie coming out of the administrative building. She looked unsettled.

"Hey," Margo called out, waving her down. "Where have you been? You won't believe what you just missed. . . ."

"I've got some bad news," Edie said glumly. "Very bad."

"What is it?" Victoria pressed, but Edie shook her head.

"I'll tell you in journalism class, along with everybody else. I don't want to have to tell the story more than once."

FIELD TRIP

ortunately, Margo and Victoria did not have long to wait; journalism was their next class. The students entered the room joking about all that had transpired that morning. Most of them would've thought it was some kind of dream had they not seen the janitor cleaning up the mess that had been created. Several students offered to help him, but he waved them off, telling them he'd been aware of the challenges of the job when he took it. Margo gave her classmates a quick explanation for what had happened, and Jory urged her to write up the story as quickly as possible.

Everyone's attention then turned to Edie, who had been silent the entire time, her expression grim.

"What's gotten into you?" Jory said. "Did you hit a brick wall with Dr. Kaboom?" As editor in chief, Jory felt it was his responsibility to take charge of things in Mr. Mister's absence. The chinless teacher hadn't been heard from since he'd bolted after his mock interview with Edie.

"It's not really about that," Edie said. "It's more about us." She took a deep breath, exhaled, then relayed her adventure. "It began with me trying to get an appointment to see Dr. Kaboom, but I was being given the runaround by his secretary, Mrs. Marblecook, who is a real cuckoo bird. I could go on and on about her, but it would take too much time, so just take my word for it. I figured out a way to get by her and into Dr. Kaboom's office. The problem was, he wasn't there. In fact, it didn't look like anybody has ever used that office for anything except maybe changing clothes. There were two full outfits in the closet, but not much else. No personal touches, no decorations or toys or pictures or papers that would give you any idea of who this guy is."

"It sounds like you searched his office," Leo said.

"Well, of course I searched his office. He wasn't there! What else was I supposed to do?"

"Wow, that's really an invasion of privacy. . . ."

"Don't you think I know that? Did you miss my campaign speech, Leo? This is who I am. I can't help myself. It's like a sickness. Now do you want to hear the story or not?" The others shouted Leo down, urging Edie to continue. She pulled her legs up so that she was sitting cross-legged in the chair.

"So that's one issue. I have no clue who Dr. Kaboom is. When you do a search for him on the Internet, nothing comes up. His credentials are suspect as well. Anyway, I happened to open a door that led to the school file room. It has files on everybody here. Don't get mad, but I looked at all of them."

"You looked in all of our files?" Aliya gasped.

"How could you do that?" Taliya chimed in. Both girls knew that in no time, the secret would be out that they'd grown up as conjoined twins—that is, freaks.

"That was really low," Ruben said. His extracurricular ballet activities would definitely be listed in that file. Good-bye, tough-guy reputation; hello, teasing.

"You're such a horrible snoop," Jory accused. Did he want people to know he had a psychiatrist on speed dial? No, he did not.

"I hate you," Victoria spat. Her excessive crying would be public knowledge in no time.

"That's going to put you on my naughty list, young lady," Santa Claus Sam said, wagging his finger sternly. "Ho ho ho."

"Oh, I suppose it's okay for me to snoop around in Dr. Kaboom's stuff, but not yours," Edie pointed out. "You guys are such hypocrites."

"I didn't say it was okay to snoop around in Dr. Kaboom's stuff—" Leo reminded her, but she interrupted him before he could finish.

"Let me assure you all that although in the past I would definitely have exploited this information, I have no intention of doing so now. I can also assure you that every one of us, including me, *every single person at this school,* has something in his or her file that makes him or her uniquely suited for Kaboom Academy."

"What do you mean?" Jory asked as the others exchanged confused glances.

"This is what I mean: we all thought we were in this school because our parents wanted an alternative to Horsemouth Middle School. That is not the case. We are at this school because we *have* to be. All of us were deemed incorrigible, unteachable, and basically undesirable. For whatever reason, we were too much of a challenge for that school, and so at the end of last year, we were all *expelled.*"

Ruben was on his feet. "They can't do that! Not unless we broke some rule . . ."

"Well, that's where they have us. Many of us, me included, did break rules, including treating people badly, jumping off buildings, being disruptive, et cetera. Others were simply too annoying to teach—Margo, Leo, Aliya, and Taliya fall into that category. They sent each of our parents a letter. I made a copy."

Edie reached into her pocket and pulled out a folded piece of paper that she handed to Jory. He read it aloud.

"'Dear Mr. and Mrs. Bickel . . .' Who is Bickel?"

"I got this from Ronny Bickel's file; he's in sixth grade," Edie explained.

"You really read everyone's file?"

"Everyone's," Edie confirmed. "Please continue."
Jory trained his eyes back on the page and started over.

Dear Mr. and Mrs. Bickel,

    After careful consideration, we have come to the difficult decision that we must excuse your child, Ronny, from further instruction at this school. His inability to sit quietly without disrupting his classes by loudly belching or passing gas every three minutes has forced us to request that you investigate other options for his education. A new private school that seeks exactly this kind of child with special needs who cannot function in a normal school setting will be opening in the fall. We hope you will take advantage of it. Meanwhile, we suggest that you not tell your child about his expulsion but instead make it seem as if the school system has somehow failed you rather than the other way around. It is important that your child approach his new school with a positive attitude.

    This decision is final, so please don't pester us with phone calls or threats of lawsuits. We have enough information on your child to bury you.

                    Yours (but not for long),
                    Principal Leonard Gravestone

"Wow," Ruben said when Jory had finished. "I know Ronny Bickel. He's a nice kid. Gassy, but nice."

"All the letters were personalized," Edie explained, "but the point is basically the same: your child is too much trouble, we don't want him around. See ya. Now, a few people's files didn't have the letter—Victoria's, for instance. . . ."

"He didn't need to send us a letter. I wasn't at Horsemouth Middle; my mom homeschooled me last year," Victoria explained.

"Yes, that's what I figured. Two of the eighth graders and four of the sixth graders also didn't have letters. They probably had similar circumstances."

"This is depressing," Jory said. More than ever, he felt like sitting on the window ledge, but it was exactly that kind of behavior that had put him in this school to begin with.

"So all of us are big fat losers," Victoria said bitterly. "And the fact that we're here means everyone knows. The administration, the teachers at Horsemouth Middle, our parents, everyone." She was surprised that she didn't feel any tears welling up in her eyes. Normally, a blow like this would send her fleeing to the bathroom, but now . . . She felt horrible but somehow she seemed to be weathering it.

"What can we do about it?" Aliya asked.

"There's nothing we can do about it," Taliya answered. "We have to accept that we were tricked."

"There is something we can do," Jory said. "We can report the truth. We may not like it, but I think every student has the right to know what's really going on."

"The truth is hard to swallow," Margo murmured.

"Well, I'd rather choke it down than live in a fantasy world," Ruben said. He turned to Edie. "You need to track down Dr. Kaboom and get that interview."

"Easier said than done," Edie replied. "I already told you, I don't think he uses that office. While his secretary was away from her desk, I looked through his appointment book. Turns out that not only did he not have any appointments, it wasn't even a real book! It was a box of chocolates disguised as a book. So I know we're all wondering the same thing. . . ."

"Yes, what kind of chocolates?" Margo blurted, then quickly added, "No, wait! I mean, where is Dr. Kaboom?"

"That's right. And this is where I'll need everyone's help," Edie said. "I found these in the pocket of one of his suits." She brought out the business cards. "They're for the Bravington Bijou," she said, handing them out to her classmates.

Leo held the card an inch away from his eyes so he could read it. "So what does this mean?"

"Why would Dr. Kaboom have so many business cards for that particular theater? My guess is that he distributes them for some reason. Maybe he's part owner of the place and wants to promote it. And if that's true, then maybe we can find him there."

Jory examined the laminated card. Edie's story had taken on a great deal of importance. It was up to him, as leader of the class, to make the decisions. He looked up, meeting the expectant gaze of his classmates, and smiled. "Tomorrow's Saturday. Anyone up for a field trip?"

• • •

The next morning all the journalism students met at the bus stop in front of the grocery store in Horsemouth, where you could take the number 9 bus to Bravington. Ruben brought the four dodgeballs, which stirred up protest from the others until he assured them he had trained the balls to behave. They had in fact become his pets, and he had even named them: Rolly, Bumpy, Whammer, and Professor Plum. "They're not bad, they're just misunderstood," he explained. Margo had brought some cinnamon rolls. She'd sprinkled them with the tiniest bit of courage, which she'd gotten from Manny "off the record." This fortified everyone's resolve. By the time the bus finally arrived, they were all eager to pursue the investigation, regardless of the danger it posed to either themselves or their grade point averages.

The Bravington Bijou was a lovely old building, built in 1904. Ornate wood carvings and brightly painted walls depicting a Parisian street theme provided whimsical décor. The theater had fallen into disrepair in the 1970s, but the Bravington Historical Society had saved it from demolition and restored it to its former beauty. It was now used for small stage shows and silent films, which rotated throughout the week.

"I've been here before, for a birthday party," Leo said to Edie as they entered the lobby. "It was a troupe of French mimes. I couldn't see what they were doing from the back row, so the other kids had to describe it to me. It sort of ruined the effect."

Ruben examined the poster propped on the easel outside the theater entrance. "There's a magician today. The Great Gumballini."

"I love magic," Margo squealed. "It's so magical."

"I know what you mean," the lumberjack, aka Sam, rumbled gruffly, swinging his axe onto his shoulder and giving Margo a wink. Margo blushed.

"We're not here to see a show," Aliya started.

"We're here to solve a mystery," Taliya ended.

"And watch where you're swinging that thing," Aliya warned.

"You nearly gave Leo a haircut," Taliya chided.

"Maybe we should ask the lady in the ticket booth if she knows anything," Victoria said, and pointed to the free-standing booth in the center of the lobby. That sounded like a good idea, so the students approached the booth.

"Can I help you?" said the ticket lady. She was actually a teenage girl with long, straight brown hair and oval glasses with white frames. Her purple sweater had a strange feather ruffle around the neck that made her look like an exotic bird.

"We're not here to buy tickets," Victoria said. "We're looking for somebody and we were hoping you could help us."

"Why should I?"

"Because . . . you have no reason not to." Victoria was afraid this would happen. Sometimes when people get a little bit of power, they like to lord it over you. Teenagers especially. "Please? We really need to find this person," she added.

"Well, I really need to sell some tickets," the girl replied tartly. "This magician is terrible. Nobody ever comes to his shows."

Jory stepped forward. "Let's make a deal. We'll buy tickets and you'll answer our questions, okay?" The girl pretended to consider it but was clearly melting under Jory's radiant charm.

"Deal," she said after a minute. "That'll be seventy-two dollars for the nine of you."

The students handed over their money and the ticket girl pointed to a jar on the counter. "Tip?" The students exchanged wary glances, but the ticket girl merely tapped the jar with her finger. "It's customary to tip someone if they give you extra service." Jory sighed, placing an extra two dollars in the tip jar. The ticket girl beamed. "Okay, so what's this person look like?"

Jory scratched his chin. "Well, he's tall and lanky, with silver hair and a mustache that curls up at the ends. He's got a handsome, lean face, but his nose is a bit big. He wears glasses with rectangular frames, and he's got funny-looking teeth. Like a horse's."

The ticket girl squinted as though she was thinking very hard but then shook her head. "Nope, can't say I've ever seen anyone who looked like that."

"Are you sure?" Victoria interjected. "He might work here or be a frequent visitor or maybe even an investor?"

"Sorry, guys, can't help you. Enjoy the show," said the

ticket girl, snapping her gum, which was the sign that the short period of her helpfulness had come to an end.

Edie glared at her. "She just ripped us off! Ruben, can't you get those balls to give her a good pounding?"

"She's pretty well protected by that booth," Ruben said. "Besides, I've rehabilitated these balls to do good, not evil."

"Well, I'm not rehabilitated," Edie muttered, noting the name tag pinned to the ticket girl's sweater. "Look out, Myrtle Brickman."

"Should we see the show?" Margo suggested.

Ruben shrugged. "We might as well. We paid for it."

"Someone's going to have to describe it to me," Leo reminded them as they entered through the double doors.

The theater space was intimate, with only a hundred chairs. They easily found seats in the front row center, as they were the only people in the audience. As soon as they sat down, the lights dimmed until the entire room was completely black. Mysterious music filled the air. After a minute or so, the lights suddenly came up, and there on the stage sat a huge treasure chest with its lid open. A small brown poodle wearing a tiny tuxedo jacket and a little top hat skipped onstage from the wings. He jumped into the box and the lid shut. In a flash the lid sprang open again, and a very tall man stood up, wearing a tuxedo and top hat. He was clean-shaven, with slick black hair and a sharp, upturned nose. Stepping from the chest, he raised his arms in exultation and proceeded to take a deep and dramatic bow as the nine audience members applauded politely. The applause turned to giggles as the little dog popped his head out of the chest and barked happily.

"He really does stink," Edie giggled to Jory as the magician slammed the lid shut.

"Ladies and gentlemen, boys and girls, I am the Great Gumballini! Welcome to my show! In the next hour you will witness illusions that will daze . . . dismay . . . and *amaze* you, as well as fantastic meats of fabric . . . *feats of magic.*"

The students were indeed amazed, but not because of the magic.

"It can't be," Margo whispered.

"But it has to be," Edie answered.

"It's him," Leo insisted. "That's his voice. How many people mangle words like that? Not many."

"This guy doesn't look anything like Dr. Kaboom," Ruben pointed out.

"Anyone can put on a costume," Aliya said.

"And a man who works in the theater would know exactly how to apply makeup convincingly," Taliya agreed.

As the students whispered among themselves, the Great Gumballini removed his hat and tapped it lightly with his wand. "Now just say the manic works—I mean, *magic words*—Abbott Costello . . . abacus dabacus . . . candelabra Santa Barbara . . ."

"Oh for Pete's sake, it's abracadabra," yelled Victoria. "And it doesn't matter what the words are, just do the trick, Dr. Kaboom!"

The Great Gumballini dropped his wand. "Who . . . who's out there?" he said, shading his eyes in an attempt to peer past the stage lights. But then the house lights came up. Jory had gotten out of his seat and turned them on.

"You are Dr. Kaboom, aren't you?" Edie accused, arms crossed.

The magician blinked his eyes. He gulped twice. "Show's over," he said, reaching into his pocket. He threw something on the ground, and the next moment a bright blue flash and a great puff of purple smoke filled the teens' vision. When the smoke cleared, the magician was gone, but the little brown poodle could be heard barking backstage, amid the clatter of running footsteps and the odd crash of props being knocked over.

"Come on!" Jory shouted, vaulting onto the stage. "He's getting away!" Everyone but Leo clambered up the steps on either side.

"I'll just stay here," Leo called, knowing he would be of little help.

"I'll watch the lobby," Sam the Lumberjack said. "In case he comes back around that way."

Everyone else fanned out backstage in pursuit of the wily magician; everyone except Edie. Edie knew that magicians, like super snoops, were experts at using trapdoors and secret hiding places. Instead of following her friends backstage, she stepped inside the chest.

Sure enough, the box had a false back that flapped down when pressed. The curtain was only a few feet away, but Edie was sure they all would have noticed it moving if the magician had escaped that way. No, there had to be some other sort of secret door. Searching the stage with her fingers, she was pleased to find a crack that gave a little when she thumped it with the heel of her hand. When she hit it hard, it swung open. Slowly, she lowered herself into the hole, her toes gingerly searching for support. She found some bars attached to a wall that served as a ladder, and she quickly climbed down.

Once Edie reached the bottom, she realized that she was in the basement underneath the stage. Though the lighting was dim, she was able to make out several other ladders that presumably led to other trapdoors. The space held a multitude of props and set pieces. A large white gazebo stood on a platform that seemed like it could be elevated onto the stage through a wide trapdoor overhead. A line of confetti cannons stood next to an antique water tank, and five large golden hoops hung on the wall. Edie could've spent hours in that room, but the barking dog reminded her of her mission and she followed the sound down a long passageway.

Edie was certain she was on the right track; as she ran, the sound of the dog got closer and closer. But her confidence faltered when she finally caught up with the pup. The poor thing had been locked in a birdcage. He pressed his furry face against the bars, trying to squeeze through, his expression desperate.

"You poor thing!" Edie unlatched the door and the dog leaped into her arms, joyfully licking her face. "Okay, okay," Edie laughed. "That's enough." She held him up in front of her, his body squirming as he strained to lick her face one more time. "I bet you hate this hat and jacket," Edie said, struggling to peel them off the wriggling animal. Indeed, the poodle looked much more comfortable unclothed. Edie sighed and put the dog down. The magician had disappeared, as magicians are known to do.

Now that the dog had stopped barking, the only sound she could hear was the stampede of her friends upstairs, still searching for the Great Gumballini backstage. She knelt down and stroked the little dog, and he quickly rolled onto his back for a belly rub.

"Do you know where your master is?" Edie said absently. The little dog rolled back to his feet and barked. Edie looked at him, amazed. "Don't tell me you understood what I said," she murmured. The little dog barked twice more, and in an instant he was off.

Edie raced after him. He turned left, then right, and then right again through the labyrinth of hallways lined with doors. They could have been storage closets, dressing rooms, or bathrooms, but Edie didn't stop to find out, instead following her adorable canine guide. Finally, he stopped outside one and sat down dutifully. He barked, scratching the door lightly with his paw. Edie took a moment to catch her breath before she pushed open the door, flicked on the lights, and gasped.

Hundreds of marionettes hung from the ceiling and lined the shelves. In Edie's opinion, there was nothing quite as creepy as a marionette. Their garishly painted faces with exaggerated features disturbed her, and the grotesque manner in which they moved, tugged by some unseen manipulator, made them appear to be hostages forced to entertain against their will. Marionettes were particularly creepy if they were like these marionettes—close to life-sized, propped in unnatural positions or swinging listlessly from their strings like recently executed criminals.

Aha! A clue! The marionettes were swinging, yet there was no open window or breeze from an air conditioner! That meant somebody had recently disturbed them, and from the direction of the swinging, that person was in the back of the room. Edie slowly made her way through the puppets, passing a king, a queen, a baker, a hunter, a genie, and a thief. On and on she went, until she finally stopped in front of a magician sitting on a crate with a very sad expression on his face.

"I found you, Dr. Kaboom," Edie said. The little dog barked gleefully, springing into a series of joyous flips. "With help from poochie here. He really likes you. Doesn't seem to want to leave your side."

"Yes, he's very needy," the magician said with a sigh, lifting him up. Immediately, the dog covered his face in slobbery kisses. "His name is PJ, though I'm thinking of changing it to Traitor." Just then, the others arrived. They had discovered the staircase that led downstairs and made a beeline for the one bright light illuminating the hallway. Edie waited patiently as the others wandered through the dangling puppets, commenting on their creepiness, until they were finally all together.

"Dr. Kaboom, we are the journalism students from Kaboom Academy," Jory began, but the magician held up his hand to silence him.

"I'm not Dr. Kaboom," he said.

"You most certainly are," Victoria asserted, holding up a silver-haired wig in one hand and a false nose and glasses with a matching silver mustache in the other. "We found this disguise in your dressing room. If you put these on, you'll look just like him."

"Don't forget the teeth," Margo said through the false teeth that she had inserted into her mouth.

"Eww, I hope you washed those first," Edie said. Margo looked startled for a moment, then quickly spit out the prosthetic piece.

"Look, it's true that I pretended to be Dr. Kablam, Ker-bloom . . . *Kaboom,* but I'm not really him. He hired me. I'm Winston Leroux, amateur magician."

"Very amateur," Ruben commented.

"It's true, I'm not very good. It's a difficult job for someone with my kind of speech imprisonment . . . *impediment.* That's why I hire myself out as an actor, to make ends meet."

"Doesn't your manner of speech also affect your acting ability?" Victoria asked.

"Yes, I'm not a very good actor either."

"Well, if you aren't Dr. Kaboom, maybe you can tell us where we can find him," Jory said. "Do you have a phone number? An address? Anything?"

"I'm afraid not. He visited me in prison . . . in *person,* in my dressing room, and gave me very strict instructions about wearing the disguise. He handed me the spinach . . . the *speeches* he wanted me to deliver, and told me to make an appearance at the school now and then so that I would be visible, but not to be too available."

"But why?" Edie persisted. "Why all the secrecy? Why

can't he just represent himself? I mean, is he some sort of monster?"

"He's an alien from another planet, isn't he," Margo whispered. "You can tell us. I know they're here. I've seen moving lights in the night sky. . . ."

Victoria put a hand firmly on Margo's shoulder. "Airplanes, Margo. Airplanes."

"He's not a monster or an alien. He's a very short man, slender, blue eyes, and balding, with a light brown mustache, though he actually has kind of a baby face. He's mild mannered, has a high voice, and is quite forgettable—you know, the kind of person who blends into the background. Of course, he could've been wearing a disguise when I met him."

Edie diligently wrote down everything Winston said. "Do you think you're going to see him again? And if so, when?"

"I don't know. He never announces when he's going to visit; he just shows up suddenly and disappears quickly. I have no idea how he gets here; he always finds me in my dressing room. I might see him if he thinks Dr. Kaboom needs to make an appearance somewhere, but I really have no idea. Now if you don't mind, I need to walk PJ. When he jumps around like that, it's not always because he's excited. Sometimes he has to go to the ballroom . . . the math room . . . the . . . ."

"We get it," Jory said. "Just take him."

Winston left the students more confused than when they had first arrived at the theater. "Does Dr. Kaboom even exist?" Aliya asked, frustrated.

"Well, somebody created the school. Somebody is behind all these crazy inventions," Taliya reasoned.

"I don't think we're going to find anything else here," Victoria said, glancing around.

"Yeah, we should go," Ruben agreed. "I have something to do this afternoon."

Edie knew it was his ballet class, but she chose not to say anything. They made their way back to the lobby, and people started to peel off. Ruben left for his class, and Aliya and Taliya had to get back to Horsemouth for a music lesson. Nobody had seen Sam leave, but Jory got a text saying that Sam's mom had come to pick him up only five minutes earlier. Leo had an eye doctor appointment. That left Edie, Victoria, Margo, and Jory.

"If you girls aren't busy, do you want to come to my house?" Jory suggested.

"Whoa, is this some kind of triple date?" Margo said.

"Uh, no. I hadn't really thought of it that way. We just need to think about our next move. Plus my mom makes terrific snacks."

Victoria shrugged. "Sure, I just have to let my mom know." The girls all pulled out their phones. Once everyone's parents had been informed, the teens headed to the bus stop, taking a short detour to get some ice cream.

RESEARCH

Jory lived in an unremarkable single-story house on the corner of two quiet streets. On the outside there was nothing fancy about it, but once you entered and went downstairs into the basement, you would discover the most fun basement in all of Horsemouth. It was a teenager's paradise, complete with a Ping-Pong table, two pinball machines, all sorts of exercise equipment, a huge television hooked up to three different game platforms and a surround-sound stereo system, and a bar stocked with peculiar sodas that Jory's mother bought from a specialty soft-drink shop. But the best thing about the room was that it was private.

The teens sat on the two sofas listening to selections from Jory's music library, which consisted mainly of movie sound tracks. They weren't talking; they were thinking. Often somebody would start to say something, then change his or her mind and stop midsentence, falling back into silence. Victoria still held the disguise, turning it over in her hands, frowning.

"I don't understand how anyone could be fooled by this

cheap thing. I mean, just look at it." She popped the wig on her head and placed the nose and glasses over her face. "This is the dumbest disguise in the world."

The others turned to glance at Victoria, but their glances turned to shocked, disbelieving stares. "What? What is it?" Victoria said nervously.

"Victoria, you look exactly like Dr. Kaboom, except for the teeth," Edie said slowly. "I mean, *exactly*."

"Oh, come on. . . ."

"I'm serious! Look."

Edie led Victoria to the mirror that hung behind the bar. Victoria gasped, staggering back slightly. She really did look just like Dr. Kaboom, except for the teeth.

"Wait a minute," said Margo, who had joined them at the mirror. Removing the false teeth from her pocket, she rinsed them off in the sink and handed them to Victoria. Victoria slid them into her mouth. Now the effect was complete.

"Hey, you know what?" Jory said finally. "That disguise reminds me of . . . it's like a Phony Face."

"What's a Phony Face?" Victoria said through the teeth.

"Yes! That's it!" Jory said, excitedly. "I knew that disguise reminded me of something when we first saw it in the theater!" Jory ran to a cabinet in the back of the room and threw open the doors, revealing several large boxes. Pulling one out, he set it on the floor and removed the lid. "They're called Phony Faces. They were advertised on the backs of comic books during the nineteen sixties and seventies. You were supposed to be able to put them on and be totally unrecognizable to your friends and family.

Here, I'll show you the ad." Jory pulled a comic from the box and brought it to the sofa. "I collect comic books."

"All of those boxes are filled with comic books?" Margo asked. "That is so cool!"

"I didn't know anyone else read comics," Jory said.

"Are you kidding? I love comics. My dad gave me his collection. He's got hundreds. . . ."

"Come on, come on, we can be rabid fans later. Right now we're trying to solve a mystery!" Edie reminded them.

"Yes, yes," Jory said. He turned the comic over to the back cover, which had a collection of very small ads under the banner "LOOK WHAT'S NEW FROM ACKERBLOOM INDUSTRIES!"

"Here it is," Jory said, pointing to one of the ads. It was a picture of a nose and glasses with a mustache and odd-looking teeth attached.

FINALLY, THE ULTIMATE DISGUISE!
Phony Face alters your appearance so no one can recognize you! Fool your family and friends as you walk among them completely unnoticed! Every Phony Face is different! Buy all twelve!!! Mix and match!!!!

"Whoever wrote that sure likes to use exclamation points," Edie commented.

"They're trying to fool kids into buying it by making it seem exciting. There were twelve different styles of beards, twelve styles of mustaches, glasses, teeth, and wigs, and you could match them up however you wanted. Anyway, my dad told me he bought a Phony Face when he was a kid but that it was just a piece of garbage. He threw it away the same day he got it."

"But this one . . . this one works," Margo said, holding up the Phony Face. "Maybe Ackerbloom Industries improved the technology."

"I don't know about that. Ackerbloom Industries went out of business years ago," Jory said. "I found out after I sent away for some rocket boots and my letter was returned to me by the post office."

"You know," Victoria said slowly, still examining the back of the comic, "there are a lot of ads for items that resemble things at school. Look at this." She held out the comic and pointed to the ad in the top right corner. "'Hypno-specs. Hypnotize your friends into believing they're anything you want them to believe.' Or this one: 'Living Balls. You would swear they were alive! Be the first kid on your block to have a ball for a pet!' 'Book in a Bite.' 'Love Potion.' We've seen all of these inventions."

Edie turned to Jory. "Do you have a computer down here? I think we should do some research on Ackerbloom Industries."

The computer was hooked up to the television, which was convenient because everybody had a good view of the huge screen. Jory typed "Ackerbloom Industries" into the search engine and instantly a list of related items appeared: *Ackerbloom Industries lawsuit, Ackerbloom Industries scandal, Ackerbloom Industries bankruptcy.*

Jory clicked on the first site, which brought up a description of the company. They all read silently for several minutes.

"So. Ackerbloom Industries was a toy company started in the nineteen fifties in upstate New York that advertised novelty items and oddball inventions on the backs of comic books," Edie summarized. "I can't believe people really bought this stuff. They must've been pretty gullible."

"Hit that link right there," Victoria directed Jory, and he did. A second article opened, showing a picture of a short, balding man with a magnificently curled mustache and beard being led away in handcuffs by police. *"George Ackerbloom Arrested for Fraud,"* the headline read. The teens scanned the story, which took a while because it was longer than the first.

"I wish I could just take this article in pill form," Edie whined. "My eyes are getting tired."

"Oh my," Margo said, still reading. "A kid was killed." The story outlined the events that took place thirty-five years earlier, when a ten-year-old boy tried to fly across a lake in an Invisiblimp, a product of Ackerbloom Industries. The Invisiblimp ad on the back of the comic promised that the individual would soar like an eagle in complete secrecy as the blimp blended into any background. Apparently, the dirigible, made of cardboard and plastic, didn't soar like anything; it sank like a stone. As it happened, the boy had been riding it over a lake when he fell. Unable to untangle himself from the soggy cardboard and plastic, he had drowned. The parents sued Ackerbloom Industries, and George Ackerbloom was charged with criminally negligent manslaughter, reckless endangerment, and fraud. The manslaughter charge didn't stick, but the endangerment and fraud charges did. He was sentenced to twenty-two years in a federal penitentiary.

"This is so sad," remarked Margo after they had finished reading.

"Wait a minute, it can't be . . . ," Edie said, staring at the photo.

"What can't be?" Margo said.

"That woman next to Ackerbloom, in the photo . . ."

"It's his wife," Victoria said, reading the caption beneath the picture. "'George Ackerbloom with lawyer Harold Rosenblatt and wife Ann-Marie.'"

"That's just it, I know her! That woman works at our school! Her name is Marianne Marblecook and she's Dr. Kaboom's secretary!"

"Wow, what a weird coincidence," Margo murmured.

"Are you sure?" said Jory, peering at the picture.

"Of course I'm sure. And by the way, she has mental problems. First of all, she's a hoarder. She was such an extreme case that she was institutionalized for it, about twelve years ago. I'm not sure how she got out, because she's still pretty kooky. Case in point, she tried to pretend she was her own identical twin, called Mrs. Cookmarble, as part of her ploy to keep me from seeing Dr. Kaboom. It was pretty ridiculous. And now that I think of it, I read an article about her that said she developed her condition after suffering a shock caused by a highly publicized scandal that ruined her family. The name didn't mean anything to me at the time, but that article probably mentioned Ackerbloom Industries."

"Who's that?" Margo rose from the couch and pointed

at someone barely visible behind Ann-Marie Ackerbloom. "It looks like she's shielding a little boy from the cameras."

"I bet it's her son," Victoria said, also rising to get a better look.

"Well, if the mother went into an insane asylum, I wonder what happened to the son?" Jory mused. There was a short pause, when suddenly Victoria's eyes widened.

"Jory, is there any paper down here?" Jory nodded, handing her a pad of yellow paper from behind the bar. Victoria immediately began writing various letters of the alphabet as though they were equations.

"This is no time for algebra," Edie chided. "We need to stay focused here."

"Not algebra, word puzzles," Victoria corrected.

"This is no time for word puzzles either."

"This is exactly the time for word puzzles," Victoria said, holding up the paper. "Look at this."

On the paper Victoria had written:

$$ANN\text{-}MARIE = MARIANNE$$
$$MARBLECOOK = COOKMARBLE$$

"See? They're anagrams. All the letters from one name are used in the other."

"That was pretty obvious to just about everyone," Edie said. "But you have to give the poor woman a break. An insane mind doesn't always come up with the best anagrams."

"No, but a clever mind can," Victoria said. "Look at this." The others huddled around her watching as she wrote:

MARBLECOOK = ACKERBLOOM

"Another anagram! Wow, good job, Victoria," said Margo, patting her on the back.

"*Great* job!" exclaimed Jory. "That can't be a coincidence. It practically proves Dr. Kaboom's secretary and this Ann-Marie Ackerbloom are the same person! Brilliant!"

"Thanks, but I'm not finished." Victoria wrote another equation.

KABOOM + X = ACKERBLOOM

"Did you notice that all the letters of 'KABOOM' are contained within 'ACKERBLOOM'? If you solve for X, the missing letters are 'C,' 'E,' 'R,' and 'L.' Let's look at those extra letters. What could they spell? Well, seeing how we're trying to figure out who Dr. Kaboom really is, let's examine his full name a little more carefully."

"It's Marcel, Marcel Kaboom," Edie said.

"Actually, it's Marcel S. Kaboom," Margo said brightly. "But we don't know what the 'S' stands for."

"It doesn't stand for anything. Look, the 'C,' 'E,' 'R,' and 'L' are all in the name MARCEL." Victoria wrote:

MARCEL S KABOOM = ACKERBLOOM + X

"Now if you solve for X . . ."

Jory sighed. "This is getting awfully math-y."

"Don't worry, we're almost done," Victoria assured him. "When you cross out all the letters that are the same on each side of the equation, you're left with three extra ones on the left: 'S,' 'A,' and 'M.'"

"Sam." Edie shrugged. "So?"

"So think about it, Edie. We happen to know a Sam, a Sam who nobody really knows anything about, a Sam who is always in costume, a Sam who has bright blue eyes just like the Great Gumballini said Dr. Kaboom had. . . ."

Edie's eyes widened. She took the pen from Victoria and slowly wrote on the paper:

$$MARCEL\ S.\ KABOOM =$$
$$SAM\ ACKERBLOOM = SAM\ BLACKMOORE$$

"Exactly," confirmed Victoria. "And he's been spying on us since school started. . . . Margo, are you okay?"

Margo's face had turned a bright shade of pink. Finding out that the object of her secret affections was a grown man made her feel a little sick. She was so glad she hadn't confided in anyone about it. "No, I'm fine, it's just a little warm in here."

"Well, get ready, because things are going to get hotter," Edie said, picking up the paper that contained Victoria's equations and scratching her chin thoughtfully. "This is going to be a very interesting interview."

SAM'S STORY

PHOTO BY LEO REISS

On Sunday all the journalism students except Sam met at the playground in Horsemouth Park, where Edie, Jory, Victoria, and Margo filled in the others on their discoveries. Victoria led them through the anagrams that indicated the likely relationship between Marcel S. Kaboom and Sam Blackmoore.

"That explains why there wasn't a file for Sam in the file room," Edie said, twirling on one of the swings. "I didn't even notice it at the time, there were so many to read, but now that I think of it, I never read his. I guess there were only fifty-four files."

"It also explains why his disguises are so good," Margo added from the swing next to Edie's. "He's been using those Phony Faces."

"And also why he doesn't take the bus," Leo said. "He's an adult. He probably drives his own car." Leo had taken a seat in the sand and was idly digging a hole with a discarded plastic shovel.

"No wonder he wanted to do the word games and puzzles for the *Daily Dynamite*," said Aliya from the high side of the seesaw.

"Word games and puzzles are his specialty!" said Taliya from the low side of the seesaw, rising as her sister sank.

"It's probably why he didn't chase the magician," Ruben mused from the merry-go-round, grabbing a bar on the large metal disk and running as fast as he could in a circle before jumping on. "Winston Leroux might have recognized him. Sam's eyes are pretty blue . . . whoaaaa!" he added, throwing back his head as he spun around.

"I feel so stupid," Victoria said, pumping her legs on the third swing. "How could I not see he was an adult? How could I be fooled so easily?"

Jory stood on top of the jungle gym, a position that would have made the others nervous if they had not already seen him in many more-precarious places. "Well, first of all, you weren't looking for it," he answered, ticking off his fingers. "Second, he looks our age. He's short and has a high voice; Winston said so. He also said Dr. Kaboom had a baby face, which probably means he can't grow a beard."

"What? What man can't grow a beard? *I'm* growing a beard," Ruben said, trying to regain his balance after rolling off the merry-go-round. "Well, not a full beard. More like a mustache."

"Yeah, right. You have a couple of hairs on your upper lip," Victoria said wryly. "Peach fuzz. My grandma has more of a mustache."

"Victoria?" Ruben staggered dizzily to the swing set, grinning broadly. "Thank you for noticing." Victoria rolled her eyes and pumped her legs harder.

"Hey, some guys can't grow beards." Jory laughed, executing a wobbly handstand on top of the monkey bars. Even though his friends weren't nervous, he did draw some worried glances from nearby parents, who quickly turned to their younger children, pointing Jory out as someone they should not emulate.

"So what are we going to do?" Edie said, still twirling on the swing. "How are we going to approach him?"

"Just walk up to him and say, 'Hey, we know who you are'?" Victoria added, stretching her legs out at the apex of her swing. She let go of the chains and flew in a wide arc before dropping to her feet without falling. "Gotcha!" she cried, grabbing the air for emphasis.

"Oh, we can have a little more fun with him than that," Jory mused, turning to Victoria. "Hey, that looked like fun. Did you feel like you were flying?"

"No, I felt like I jumped off a swing," Victoria said. "But it was fun."

Everyone switched places. Jory leaped off the jungle gym and sat on the swing, pumping his legs as hard as he could, competing with Victoria and Ruben to see who could jump the farthest. Aliya and Taliya spun each other on the merry-go-round while Edie and Margo mounted the seesaw. Leo's hole had gotten so big he could sit inside it, which he did, though he gave it up to swing, something that was fun even if you couldn't see very well. For the rest of the afternoon, the group played in the park. For so long they had considered it to be a place where only little kids played; they'd forgotten how much fun little kids have. As they played they continued to discuss the recent events and how to trip up Sam. By the time the streetlights turned on, they had formulated their plan.

• • •

The next day the journalism students went through all their classes without saying anything about their discovery. If Sam figured out that they were on to him, he might disappear, and they'd never have their questions answered. Finally, at the end of the day, during journalism class, Jory called a meeting.

"Okay, everyone," he said. "Since Mr. Mister is no longer here, I thought I should check in and see how your stories are coming along. Victoria?"

"My rewrite is almost done," she said.

"Margo?"

"I'll have a first draft by the middle of the week."

"Ruben?"

"Mine's done. I made all your changes."

"Aliya and Taliya?"

"We're also done. We're thinking of taking a poll on the dress code."

"Excellent. Leo, how are you doing on photographs?"

"They're all done. I emailed them to you. At least, I think I did . . . I couldn't see the buttons very well. I might have deleted them instead."

"Don't worry, we'll find them. How about you, Edie?"

"I still haven't managed to track down Dr. Kaboom," she said with a sigh. "After hitting that dead end on Saturday, I'm thinking of just giving up. I mean, there's nothing on this guy. I have a feeling he doesn't even exist. He's just a con artist, pretending to be someone he isn't. Why, he's nothing but a big fat fraud, *just like his dad.*"

The sultan with the bright blue eyes leaped to his feet. "You take that back! My dad was not a fraud! He was a genius!" Almost immediately, the sultan knew he'd said too much. His mouth hung open as he slowly began backing away. Turning around, he bolted for the door, only to discover Victoria and Margo blocking it.

"Sorry, no exit," Victoria said.

Sam's eyes darted from one student to another as they closed in on him. Then, much to everyone's surprise, he sprang into the air, deftly flipping himself so that his hands and feet hit the ceiling, where he stuck like a giant gecko.

"How'd he get up there?" Aliya gasped.

"He's got springs on his shoes," Taliya pointed out.

"They're called Boing-Boing Boots," said Jory. "And he's wearing Sticky Mitts on his hands and knees so he can cling to any surface! They're advertised on the back of another comic book!"

"Explain it later," Edie interrupted. "He's getting away!"

Sure enough, Sam was padding along the ceiling,

heading toward the skylight. The ceilings were twelve feet up, much too high for the students to reach no matter how athletic they were. Ruben executed one of his pirouettes, snatching Sam's cape from his shoulders. It wasn't enough to bring him down, but the jump reminded him that he had friends who could reach even higher. Ruben gave a sharp whistle. The balls rolled out from under his seat, where they liked to cuddle by his feet. Ruben pointed to Sam. "Fetch!"

Starting low, the balls began building up momentum and altitude with each bounce. Higher and higher and higher they went, until one of them knocked off Sam's turban. The next ball slammed Sam in the head and bit off his wig, revealing that he was, in fact, bald. The balls became increasingly excited, wildly caroming off the wall, floor, and ceiling with such speed that the students had to duck under the tables to avoid being hit themselves.

Still the balls were not able to break Sam's grip. He grunted as they smacked against him, but he managed to slowly crawl to the skylight in the ceiling. When he pressed the Boing-Boing Boots against the window, the powerful springs hidden within the soles punched the skylight out with a loud thump, sending it flying over the roof.

"Oh no!" Aliya cried.

"He's going to the roof!" Taliya wailed.

"So? What's he going to do up there? He can't possibly jump," Victoria said.

Sam hoisted himself out the window. Just before he disappeared, one of the balls hit him in the nose, and the sultan Phony Face fell off. Edie ran to pick it up. In her hands the disguise looked cheap and ridiculous, an angular nose with a long black mustache and an even longer beard, split in half at the bottom. Jory had opened the window on the wall closest to the skylight. Sticking his head out, he craned his neck to view the roof.

"I can get up there," he said confidently.

"Jory, no . . . ," Leo said, but it was too late. Jory was already on the ledge. In the next instant he was climbing up the side of the building. The others stuck their heads out and watched him ascend, marveling at his ability to find and grasp the narrow fingerholds and toeholds between the bricks, praying that he didn't fall. Reaching the gutter downspout, Jory grabbed onto it and used it to climb the rest of the way, as quickly as a monkey scrambling up a coconut tree.

"He made it! Jory's on the roof!" Ruben yelled. "Come on!"

Ruben charged out of the room with his classmates close on his heels. They found the only staircase that had roof access, but it was locked. "Balls! Open!" Ruben ordered. The four balls gave themselves three practice bounces, and then all four came together in a powerful blast against the target, *BOOM!* The door flew open and the students charged up the steps.

Meanwhile, Jory was in hot pursuit of a short, balding man whom he had known as Sam but who apparently was the headmaster of the school, Dr. Kaboom. Jory had trouble keeping up; after all, Sam had gotten a substantial head start. But Jory figured he didn't have to hurry since Sam was quickly running out of room on the rooftop. There were no buildings close enough to reach by jumping, and Jory didn't believe Sam intended to commit suicide.

And yet Sam wasn't slowing down. He was heading right for the edge at full speed. Then, off in the distance, the horizon seemed to shift ever so slightly. Jory blinked. Then it happened again. The scenery beyond the school moved and then corrected itself. Jory stopped running. He shook his head and rubbed his eyes. Was he dizzy? No, he seemed to be fine. The building under him wasn't moving either. He turned around, checking the other directions— south, west, north. . . . It was only the eastern horizon that kept moving. And still Sam was running straight toward that ever-shifting scenery.

In a flash Jory realized what was happening. He laughed, and then increased his own speed, sprinting as fast as he could, as Sam dove forward and disappeared.

Ruben burst through the door on the rooftop and saw his friend racing toward the edge of the building. "Jory! Stop!" he cried. The others emerged from the staircase just in time to see Jory take a flying leap and vanish over the side. Margo and Edie screamed. Aliya and Taliya were stunned into speechlessness. Victoria couldn't help herself; she started to cry. Ruben rushed to the building's edge, not willing to believe what his eyes were telling him, that Jory had finally lost his mind and jumped off the roof.

Then he backed up. Rising from the edge of the building was a strange oblong inflated object that looked very much like a miniature blimp, except this blimp blended in so perfectly with the sky that it was practically invisible. All he could see was a thin oval outline, detectable only by a slight delay in the mechanism creating this amazing visual effect.

Beneath the blimp hung a compartment large enough for perhaps two children or one small adult. The same sort of invisibility mechanism cloaked the compartment; however, the compartment was made more obvious by the boy dangling from its open window: Jory. Sam could be seen through the opening arguing with him, but after a short exchange, he grabbed Jory's arms and helped him inside. Slowly, the blimp lost altitude, sinking toward the courtyard.

That is what Ruben saw. Jory, however, knew perfectly well as he made his dive over the side of the building that he was not on a suicide mission. He had recognized the Invisiblimp from the advertisement on the back of his comic books. As it rose slowly before him, he made a quick calculation of its distance, his speed, his jumping ability, and his strength, and once he made that calculation, he knew that this was the opportunity he'd been waiting for all his life. He sprinted toward the edge of the building, feeling no fear, only excitement. He pushed off the edge of the roof, lunging for the passing window with complete focus, like an arrow heading for a target. His fingers grabbed the window opening perfectly. He felt gravity jolt his body as he slammed against the compartment, but he had strong arms and knew he could hang on. Jory had, in fact, practiced for just this sort of situation using the chin-up bar in his bedroom doorway.

Sam immediately appeared at the window, shouting that their combined weight was too much for the Invisi-blimp to bear. For a moment Jory feared that Sam would peel his fingers away from the windowsill one by one until he plummeted to his death, but fortunately, Sam was no villain. Jory felt a great deal of relief when Sam helped him inside.

As they drifted downward, Sam showed Jory how to work the Invisiblimp, how to steer it, how to make it accelerate, and how the cloaking mechanism worked, though the science behind it was much too advanced for Jory to fully comprehend. By the time they landed, the rest of the journalism class, along with the balls, were there to meet them. Jory threw open the compartment door, euphoric.

"Did you see that? Did you see it? For a second there I was flying! Oh man, there is nothing like it! It was . . . it was . . . *glorious!*"

"You idiot!" Victoria strode up to Jory, punching him hard on the shoulder. "You scared us!"

"I did?"

"Of course you did!" Aliya blurted.

"We thought you were dead!" Taliya added.

"Don't you know we care about what happens to you?" Margo said.

"I don't know what they're talking about; that was pretty awesome, dude," Ruben said.

"I didn't see it," Leo said. "But I got some pictures anyway."

"What about Dr. Kaboom?" Edie said. They all turned to the Invisiblimp, which was now blending in perfectly with the surrounding grass of the courtyard. Sam had stepped out of the compartment and immediately the balls circled him threateningly.

"Call off the balls, Ruben," Sam said sadly. "I'm not going anywhere."

Ruben gave a sharp whistle. The balls stopped circling and bounced happily into the compartment, perhaps to explore; nobody was sure what the balls might want in there. But the teens had bigger issues at hand than figuring out the peculiar interests of dodgeballs.

"May I have my interview now, Dr. Kaboom?" Edie asked.

"Yes, but please, don't call me Dr. Kaboom. It's Sam Ackerbloom. Dr. Kaboom is just one of my inventions . . . but I think you already know that."

The journalism students followed Sam into his office in the administration building, passing Mrs. Marblecook, who had created an interesting tower out of several hundred Wite-Out bottles.

"Hi, Mom," Sam said as he passed her. Mrs. Marblecook just waved and went back to her project.

Once they had all gathered in his office, Sam closed the door. "Sorry I ate all the chocolates in your appointment book," Edie admitted.

"That's all right," Sam said, gesturing to the sofa and chairs, indicating that the students should sit. Four of them wedged themselves onto the sofa. Edie settled in the armchair with Victoria, and Jory perched next to her on the wide armrest. Leo sat on the floor, trying to figure out where to point the camera. Sam took his place behind the desk, facing them.

It was obvious to the students, seeing Sam for the first time without the phony face or a costume, that he was not a teenager. His thinning light brown hair revealed a shiny bald spot, and a crinkle around his eyes betrayed his age. Still, he looked young for a middle-aged man. He was a little more than five feet tall—Edie's height—and slender. His face was cherubic, and his eyes were so big and bright he resembled a baby. Sitting there at the desk, he looked like a kid making believe he was an adult.

The students sat in silence, all thinking pretty much the same thing: if they thought Sam looked ridiculous before in all of his costumes, he looked just as ridiculous now as a real person. But Edie had been waiting for this moment for a week. Finally, she could confront the man who had been evading her.

"Dr. Kaboom . . . ," she began, "or should I call you Mr. Ackerbloom?"

"Please, call me Sam. After all this time I feel like we're friends."

"Friendship is based on honesty and trust," Victoria interrupted. "Which I'm afraid you have not demonstrated."

Sam bit his lip. Edie almost felt sorry for him. Almost.

"All right, Mr. Liar, why don't you tell us how you came up with this dastardly middle school scheme?"

"Dastardly? Scheme? You make it sound dishonest."

"Hello? It is dishonest! You hired somebody to play a fictional character with made-up credentials. You totally misrepresented yourself to our parents. You pretended to be a very weird kid just to spy on us. You hired unlicensed, inexperienced teachers, some of whom I believe were inmates at this facility when it was a madhouse."

"Patients. They're called patients. And it was an asylum."

"Whatever. And you are using highly questionable teaching materials that are nothing more than your father's fraudulent inventions. . . ."

Sam jumped to his feet. "Those inventions were not fraudulent!" he declared, his face turning red.

"Sit down, Sam," Ruben cautioned. "The balls don't like sudden movements. Sure enough, the four balls had bounced in through the open window and were clustered warily around Ruben's feet. He patted them gently until they calmed themselves and rolled behind him.

"We've got you, Mr. Ackerbloom," Edie said. "The jig is up. Once we print this story, you'll be finished. Done. Through. But we only have half the story; we need your side. It's our obligation as journalists to report everything and not hold anything back. Mr. Mister may have been crazy, but he was right about that. So if you would, just start at the beginning. It will save me having to ask a lot of pointless questions. Spill." Edie poised her hand over her notebook, her pen at the ready.

Sam closed his eyes as the students shifted around in their seats, uncomfortable in the silence. Even the balls bumped against the wall impatiently. Finally, after a full minute passed, Sam opened them and spoke.

"When I was growing up, I thought my dad was the greatest man in the world," he began. "George Ackerbloom dreamed up some of the most amazing inventions. Many of them didn't have any point except to be used for fun, to make you laugh, just some odd piece of whimsy. That's what he thought, anyway, but for the kids who played with them, the toys were keys to unexplored worlds, passports to exciting adventures . . . they were the sparks that lit the imagination."

"But they didn't work," interrupted Leo.

"They *did* work!" Sam jumped up from his seat, slamming his hand on the desk as he did so. "They did! The problem is, nobody ever read the instructions!" He noticed the balls becoming visibly agitated and sat down again.

"Why would people not read instructions?"

"People never read instructions, not well. Maybe they're in too much of a hurry or maybe they don't think it's necessary or maybe the writing is too small or they just get so excited about the toy that they don't even bother to look for instructions. But the fact is, if you followed the instructions, my father's inventions *did* work. They worked perfectly. Dad got blamed for his own customers' oversight. People called his inventions junk. But because they were so inexpensive, nobody bothered to ask for a refund. If they had, my father would have sent them another set of instructions or he would've replaced the item. Dad was a good businessman. Customer satisfaction was important to him. He didn't know the extent to which people considered his inventions to be worthless until . . . well, until the accident."

"You mean the drowning," prompted Edie.

"Yes," Sam said with a sigh. "That had to be the worst day of his life. It tore my dad apart. He was never the same again. And that poor kid . . . well, I was seven at the time so I don't remember exactly what happened, just that once again nobody had read the instructions that would've told them how to make the Invisiblimp waterproof. Nobody read about the life vest and the shoe-chute tucked in their compartments in case of emergency—"

"Shoe-chute? What's that?" Jory interrupted.

"It's a parachute that comes out of your shoes. You hold on to the cords and balance upright. You're supposed to put them on before you start flying. It makes landing much easier than the typical backpack-style parachute."

"Can I have one?"

"Jory, focus," Victoria reprimanded. "Edie, continue."

Edie nodded. "So then there was a lawsuit, and George Ackerbloom was convicted and sent to prison."

"He was sentenced to twenty-two years. I never saw him after that. My life changed completely. Right after the trial, a mob of people showed up at Ackerbloom Industries. They were furious that the murder charge hadn't stuck. They torched the place. It went up like a huge bonfire. But the thing was, we lived at that factory, in a suite of rooms over the factory floor. My mom and I . . . we lost everything—all the inventory, all of our stuff, our furniture, clothes, keepsakes . . . *everything*. That's when my mom snapped. She started keeping everything that came into her possession. She couldn't let anything go. . . . I don't know, maybe she was trying to replace what she'd lost. And she never took me to see my dad in prison because she didn't want me to think of him as a criminal. I wrote him letters, though, and he always wrote back. He regretted that he was not there to raise me, and that our name would forever be stained by scandal. In his last letter he begged me to be strong and not let his fate affect my own. I was fourteen when he died in prison.

"As you can probably guess, I did not have a happy childhood with a father behind bars. Because the entire country had heard of the scandal, right after the trial, Mom and I legally changed our name to Marblecook, an anagram I came up with in honor of my dad's love of puzzles, and we moved to Horsemouth to get away from everything. Horsemouth is a good place to hide. Nothing happens here. Nobody would ever suspect any resident of being famous, or infamous, as the case may be. I went through the Horsemouth school system, which was not a good experience for me. And though we were trying to blend in and pretend we were just as boring and bland as everyone else, my mother's mind was slowly deteriorating. She kept collecting and collecting. She amassed so much junk I moved into my tree house. I set up a cot and sleeping bag and kept my clothes in a big suitcase."

"Did her friends really get lost in that mess?" Edie whispered.

"Yes, but don't worry, they all made it out alive. I finished high school as quickly as I could so that I could move out and get away from all that clutter. I was so happy when I finally left for college. . . ."

"Right. College. I'd love to read your thesis paper on learnomology, thinkonomics, and edumechanics," Victoria interjected wryly.

"Ah, yes. Well, I did make that up. I didn't major in any of those things. I went to a small technical school in Canada that I doubt you've heard of and majored in mechanical engineering and industrial design with a minor in education. I was thinking about becoming a physics teacher, but at the same time, I was reluctant to become part of an institution that was so pedantic, so bereft of fun and joy. It was around this time that I started toying with the idea of creating a school where I *would* want to teach, and better yet, a place where I would want to learn. I spent hours daydreaming about the physical structure, the courses, the teachers. . . . Of course, at this point it was hypothetical. It would be years before I could make it a reality."

"Jump ahead, then," Edie ordered. "Where did you get the money to create Kaboom Academy?"

"I won the lottery. Literally. About ten years ago I was just bumping around in my thirties, living in upstate New York, and I was at a really low point. My mom had just been institutionalized two years earlier, right here, actually. As you know, this property used to be an insane asylum, quite a nice one in fact."

"Yes, Mr. Mister gave us the first clue, and your mom pretty much confirmed it," Jory said. "But please, continue."

"Well, nice or not, I still felt guilty for abandoning her. On top of that, I'd been trying to develop a line of educational toys, things I'd devised from my daydreams, but nobody was interested in my ideas, and I was quickly getting nowhere. I moved back here, to Horsemouth, so that I could be closer to my mom, and took a tedious job drafting designs for kitchen appliances. At this point I was just trying to make ends meet so that I could afford to keep Mom at this facility, which, being private, was quite expensive. And I didn't want to have to sell her house. Not that I wanted to live there—it was still brimming with office supplies—but I knew if I sold that place it would break her heart. Anyway, one day I went into a convenience store and bought some nachos, a copy of *Scientific American,* and a lottery ticket. Two days later I was worth fifty million dollars."

"If this place was such a great asylum, didn't you feel bad about taking it away from those patients?" Margo piped up.

"I didn't take it away. I merely bought it from the owners, Dr. Harper and Dr. Friedkin, two psychiatrists in their late seventies who wanted to retire. They were looking for a buyer; I was looking for a campus. They had already transferred the tough cases out in anticipation of their departure; the rest of the patients were here on a volunteer basis, by a doctor's recommendation, not a court order. Most of those people are still here. They're the staff and faculty of Kaboom Academy."

"Omigosh! Don't you think that was pretty irresponsible?" Aliya squealed.

"They have no formal training!" Taliya added.

"That made them perfect for the job! I didn't have to retrain them or change their ways. Besides, no professionally trained teacher in his right mind would agree to teach at a school using my materials and methods. The obvious solution was to find teachers that weren't in their right mind. Lucky for me, there was no shortage of patients here with advanced degrees who were up to the task and eager to work! In fact, many of them are improving. Having a useful purpose is wonderful therapy, and working with teens, who, let's admit, are naturally nuts, allows them to see that compared to their students, they're not so crazy after all."

"Really. And their families agreed to this?" Edie pressed.

"Absolutely! Their families were all for it. The patients still get the psychiatric care they need—we call the sessions 'staff meetings.' They're held in the auditorium, led by the school nurse and the school psychologist, who are both licensed for that work. The only real difference, and it's a big one, is that instead of playing backgammon and watching TV in their free time, they have something far more interesting and important to do: educate our youth. That's what you call a real win-win situation!"

"What about Mr. Mister? He fell off the deep end. We haven't seen him since Edie's interview," Margo reminded him.

"Actually, he's hiding in the gardening shed," Ruben said. "The balls found him a couple of days ago. I tried to get him to come back to class, but he just kept nodding and saying he didn't want to buy my cookies. I think he'd put both his earplugs back in."

"Ah yes, poor Mr. Mister was driven crazy by his unfortunate name. If only his parents had named him something like Jack or Fred, but no, their nasty sense of humor doomed him to a lifetime of teasing, the result being that he's quite . . . eccentric, shall we say? Nice guy, though, and a good teacher. Would you believe he has a master's degree in the classics? Greek and Latin."

"We have veered way off the course," Edie said, becoming impatient. "Go back to the scandal. You keep avoiding it."

"Edie, I revisit that scandal every day of my life. I grew up living under that shadow of shame. As a seven-year-old child, I hated my dad for what he'd done, but later, when I realized it wasn't entirely his fault, I eventually forgave him. And then I went one step further. I decided to redeem him, to repair his reputation by making all of his inventions idiotproof, so that even if you didn't read the instructions, the inventions would work. Once I became independently wealthy, I was able to dedicate all of my time to this, and I'm happy to say, I've succeeded. And it is a happy coincidence that many of my father's devices have turned out to be excellent teaching tools."

"Not entirely," Victoria said. "Those book pills made me sick to my stomach."

"Well, you're right. That's why I was very clear that this is an experimental school and that my methods may need modification. Those book pills are a good example. Clearly, taking them all at once is a very bad idea. Because of your experience, I know I should now package them differently, so that the pills' casings remain locked until the appropriate date. I should stamp the name of the book directly on the pill, not on the packaging. That was very helpful, so thank you."

"You should do both," suggested Leo. "But please remember to stamp the name of the books in very large print."

"Absolutely!"

"So we really are just an experiment," Aliya murmured.

"Like bacteria in a petri dish." Taliya sighed.

"After all, we are the rejects from the other school," Edie reminded them. She turned to Sam. "I guess you thought since we were totally undesirable you could do whatever you wanted with us."

"Not so!" Sam protested. "Not at all. First, you are not rejects to me. I picked each of you specifically to be in this school."

"Please! You know perfectly well that I saw everyone's file! We all had the same horrible expulsion letter from the principal at Horsemouth Middle School."

"Well, in truth, I asked Leonard Gravestone to write those letters. I told him that I planned to create a private school but that I didn't want to compete with the Horsemouth public schools. I said, 'Give me the kids you don't want, your toughest-to-teach students, the worst of the worst—"

"You know, if you're trying to suck up to us, you're doing a terrible job," Victoria snapped.

"Don't you understand? You're not the problem! My entire early childhood was about building, creating, exploring, *learning* . . . and it was all fun. My dad and I spent hours tinkering and making things that had no other purpose than to be interesting. Outsiders might think we were engaged in idle nonsense, but I learned so much about the world in those carefree days, more than most people learn in a lifetime.

"When my father went to prison, I went from being taught at home by my parents to having to attend regular school. It was then that I entered a world of rigidity. Fun was confined to fifteen minutes at recess and a half hour during lunch, and even then you were told where to play and what to play and with whom you could play. Classes were the same. You were told what you would learn, when you would learn it, and at what point you would move on to the next subject. You learned by reading and memorizing. People with excellent memories did well. People with bad memories, or who didn't have the patience for or interest in memorization, did poorly. And then came those awful labels: gifted, slow, disruptive, teacher's pet, prepared, disorganized, quiet, socially awkward. . . . It was like they had to put each student in a tidy little box, labeled and shelved. But there's no room to grow in that box, and no matter how hard you try, those labels don't peel off!"

The teens nodded. All of them had at one time suffered from being labeled.

"Well, personally, I hate labels," Sam continued. "They keep you from growing and changing and becoming what you want to be. You're trapped in other people's expectations. . . . But don't get me started on this; it's a subject on which I can become quite passionate."

"But this is exactly what we're talking about," Edie reminded him.

"Oh yes, that's right." Sam laughed. "Anyway, the point is, I'm one of you. I started this school for kids who were just like me, who for whatever reason didn't fit into a little box. That's why I approached Principal Gravestone. I also spread around a lot of flyers advertising Kaboom Academy, just to make sure I got the kids who weren't in the public school but who still fit the profile of the kind of student I sought. That's how I got Victoria, for instance."

Edie held up her hand; she'd heard enough. "Look, you talk a good game, I'll give you that, Sam, if that's your real name. . . ."

"It is my real name."

"But the fact is that this school is built on a sham. If it weren't, you wouldn't have to be so sneaky about it. Why couldn't you just present yourself as the headmaster of the school, using your real name, instead of hiring some cut-rate magician to play some fake person with a made-up name? Why couldn't you try to hire real teachers instead of crazy people—I know, I know . . . *patients*. Why couldn't you work in this office and do the sorts of things a real head of school does, instead of pretending to be a student? We trusted you! And what about poor Margo? She had a crush on you!"

"Edie! I did not. . . . I never . . . ," Margo protested lamely, betrayed by her bright pink face.

"We shared things with you that we would never have

shared with an adult! And the whole time you were just studying us, taking notes. I've never felt so . . . so violated!" Edie was able to articulate these charges with ease, for she had often been on the receiving end of such speeches. Now that she was a victim, it made her furious.

"I'm sorry, but I had to pretend to be a student," Sam explained. "I had to see how things were operating from a kid's point of view. If something wasn't working, I needed to know. I wanted to hear your honest opinions."

"Well, this is our honest opinion: you stink, Sam Ackerbloom, and your whole school stinks. I'm going to write this story and I'm revealing everything. And I'll tell you something else. This story is big. It's huge. It's almost too important for the *Daily Dynamite*. Wait, did I say 'almost'? It *is* too important for the *Daily Dynamite*! This story is going straight to the *Horsemouth Hornblower* . . . and also to the *Bravington Bugle*! I'm busting this operation wide open! And it's all coming down!"

EDIE'S STORY–PART TWO

die sat in front of her computer, fingers tingling. She had covered the desk with all of her notes, but she didn't need them. Every fact was seared into her memory, and pretty soon they would be spread all over the front page of every newspaper in New Hampshire. When she'd told Sam that this story would make the front page of the *Horsemouth Hornblower*, she wasn't kidding. In a town like Horsemouth, where a cat having kittens is considered news and somebody backing into a mailbox and not leaving a note is the crime of the century, a scam perpetrated upon fifty-five Horsemouth families by a master of disguise with a scandalous past would be the biggest thing to hit the town since . . . well, since the school itself.

She cracked her knuckles and rested her fingertips on the computer keyboard, trying to think of how to begin. There were so many elements to include. First, the school itself, with all of its oddities: the teachers, the classes, the teaching methods, and the atmosphere. Most people wouldn't believe it. They would think she was describing a circus, a dream, a hallucination. And then there was the whole history of the creation of Kaboom Academy, George Ackerbloom's scandal, Sam's mother's institutionalization, Sam's own rocky school experience. That also had to be explained. And finally, the craftiness of the scam itself: Sam's disguising himself as a student and hiring a magician to play Dr. Kaboom, a man fabricated out of nothing but nonsense. Getting Principal Gravestone to expel them from Horsemouth Middle School. Scamming parents at the introductory meeting to get them to sign up. Experimenting on the students with his "improved" inventions . . . for what purpose? So that he could create more Kaboom Academies? Collect more unwanted students on which to experiment? And what would their parents think once they discovered what was really going on? Sure, they knew what little their children had told them about the school, but they didn't know the whole story. Certainly, once they found out, they would be mortified, ashamed that their desperation blinded them to such a swindle. Well, that was the price they'd have to pay. Once her story hit the presses,

Sam Ackerbloom would be through. Kaboom Academy would shut down and Horsemouth Middle School would be forced to rescind the phony expulsions. Then it would be back to business as usual. . . .

Edie felt a weight land in her stomach with a sickening thud. Back to business as usual? Business as usual at Horsemouth Middle School was horrible! It was boring! It was frustrating! It was certainly nothing to which she wanted to return. The only thing she learned there was how to please teachers by memorizing what they said and spitting it back at them. And socially, she was an outcast. Nobody dared get anywhere near her for fear that she would gather information and use it against them.

Edie had never wanted to be a gossip. She didn't particularly enjoy hurting people. It was just that two years earlier, when her family had first moved from Manhattan to Horsemouth, she had been lonely. This town was so quiet and dull. She was used to the fast-paced energy of the city, not the torpor of a remote suburb. Because she didn't have any siblings and her parents were always so busy, there was nobody to talk to. She tried to make friends with some girls down the block, girls who she knew were considered popular, but they weren't very kind. Apparently, she wasn't wearing the right shoes, or was it jeans? Or maybe she was wearing her hair the wrong way. Whatever the problem was, it was trivial. Nevertheless, Edie knew if she was going to succeed socially, she would have to watch closely, listen carefully, and copy what the other girls did.

As Edie watched and listened, it began to dawn on her that these girls weren't as perfect as they claimed to be. Each one had faults. Each one had secrets. It delighted Edie that deep down, these popular girls were just as self-conscious and anxious as she was; they just weren't admitting it. A few months later, she tried approaching this same social group a second time, now matching their dress and mannerisms, but it didn't work. They rejected her again. They were so mean! They were so insulting! Edie couldn't believe these girls would behave that way, knowing what she knew about them . . . and that was when she understood the power she possessed. She could stop their tyrannical reign over the school. No longer would students have to endure their hurtful snubs and abuse. Surely that would gain her the appreciation and respect of her peers. So Edie revealed all, blabbing every single piece of embarrassing information she had gathered about the girls.

Only it didn't turn out the way she'd hoped. Instead of the other kids raising her up on their shoulders, they feared her. They avoided her even more than before. At the same time, Edie had become addicted to information. The more the other kids refused to interact with her, the harder she worked to find out everything about them. If anyone treated her badly, she'd leak what she'd learned, leaving her target a blubbering mess of shame and humiliation.

Things went from bad to worse after that. Nobody was safe, not even adults. Edie knew she was out of control. She only pretended to be proud of what she'd accomplished—splitting up friendships, getting people fired, and the like. In fact, she sorely regretted it. The problem was, she couldn't stop; she had become too good at gossiping. It was now second nature; she could do it in her sleep. And so Edie had become exactly the thing she hated most of all: a malicious monster.

But at Kaboom Academy, despite her overt spying, she'd actually made . . . were they friends? Yes, they were. They might not have started out that way, but somewhere in all the craziness the kids in the journalism class had bonded. Not only that, they had changed. Edie looked at her computer screen, where she had yet to type in a single word. She decided to phone a friend.

• • •

Victoria arrived with Margo and Jory. When Edie had called Victoria, Margo was at her house; they both decided to call Jory because he was the editor in chief. Jory showed up with Leo and Ruben and one of the dodgeballs (the other three balls had something else to do that day), and since everyone else was there, Edie called Aliya and Taliya. Fortunately, the twins lived just down the block, so it didn't take long for them to arrive. Mr. and Mrs. Evermint were thrilled that so many young people were at their house and that none of them seemed to be upset with Edie. Mrs. Evermint quickly whipped up a batch of brownies to celebrate the occasion.

"I just can't write this article knowing that it's going to destroy the school," Edie explained to the others. They were all sitting on the back porch, looking out at the Evermints' lovely garden, munching on brownies and sipping lemonade. "I thought I wanted to expose Sam Ackerbloom because I feel what he did was wrong, but . . . I mean, do you guys want to go back to the way things were? Can you even imagine?"

Victoria pushed the rocker back and forth with her heels. "Well, I probably wouldn't go back to being homeschooled;

my mom is still working. To tell you the truth, the reason I wasn't enrolled at Horsemouth Middle was because . . . I had this sort of problem controlling my emotions. But that seems to be gone now. So I'm pretty sure I would be okay."

"And I think I could turn my reputation around," Margo said, delicately trying to sit in the hammock. "I don't say nearly as many boneheaded things as I used to. . . . WHOA!" She flipped out of the swinging seat, landing on her rear end.

"I still want to fly," Jory admitted, diving into the now-empty hammock with ease. "In fact, I had an awesome flying dream last night. It was weird, though. I was flying over these fields, and then I noticed that beneath me was the school bus. The windows to the bus opened and all the students, including you guys, climbed onto the roof. The bus was still moving! And then you lifted your arms and everyone started to rise, and then we were all flying together. And when we got to the school, everyone was zooming around it, in and out windows . . . like some crazy sort of hive."

"That's . . . pretty cool, actually. But I still can't write the story," said Edie, throwing up her hands.

"I think this is what they call a conflict of interest," Victoria said between bites of brownie. "You're tempted to hold back the truth because the possible outcome would affect you negatively."

"Not just me, everyone," Edie corrected her. "I just don't want to destroy Kaboom Academy. I don't care about Ackerbloom; I care about us. That school is the best thing that's ever happened to us!"

"You know, I think I see the problem," Ruben said. "The reason you can't write the story is because you're missing something. Let's go back to the basics: *who, what, when, where, why.*"

"*Who* is Sam Ackerbloom," Edie said.

"*What* is that he created a school under false pretenses," Victoria said.

"*When* is last summer, leading up to right now," Aliya said.

"*Where* is here in Horsemouth," Taliya said.

"*Why* . . ." Margo stopped. "I don't know," she admitted. "Usually somebody runs a scam to make money. But this school is free."

"Sam said he created the school to redeem his father's name," Leo said helpfully.

Jory frowned. "Redeem?" Then he smiled. And laughed. "I know why Sam's doing it. He said it right at the beginning of the school year, or rather the fake Dr. Kaboom did. Edie, the reason you can't write the story is your claim is all wrong. The school *isn't* a scam; it is doing exactly what he said it would. I'm sorry, but you'll have to scrap everything you've done so far. You have a whole new story to write."

"I already deleted my first attempt," Edie admitted. "And for this second version, the only thing I've written is the headline, 'Private School Scam Astounds Community.' Consider it scrapped. What's the new story?"

Jory rolled out of the hammock deftly and sat next to Edie. "*Who* is us, the students of Kaboom Academy. *What* is the creation of a new school with the strangest teaching methods, staff, and curriculum known to mankind. *Where* is Horsemouth, New Hampshire, but hopefully it will spread. *When* is now. *Why?* To redeem *us*. But more importantly, to make us vigorous citizens of the world, madly in love with learning!"

THE STORY OF THE CENTURY

On November 4, the very first issue of the Kaboom Academy *Daily Dynamite* was distributed around the school. The few kids who read it enjoyed the articles, which explained the idea behind all of the strange things they had been experiencing in their classrooms. They laughed at the poll about the dress code, snickered at the comic, worked out the crosswords, and puzzled over the photographs. When they got to the final page and read the article about the founder of the school, however, many of them were stunned. They quickly gathered their friends who hadn't seen the paper and prompted them to read it. By lunchtime, classrooms were abuzz with the news; nobody got any work done, and every student took a copy of the paper home.

It took only a day for all of Horsemouth to find out about the article. Horsemouth was a small town where gossip spread quickly, especially when nobody's cat had birthed a litter of kittens recently. Men and women flocked to their favorite community establishments. Bars had big business. The hair salons and barbershops were packed too. Office watercooler bottles were drained as quickly as they were replaced, as workers crowded around them to chew on the juiciest piece of information they'd heard in years. And the phone lines were busier than ever before.

The following morning Sam sat in his office, staring out the window at all the students, their noses buried deep in the newspaper. Every once in a while somebody would look up and point in his direction, and he would look away. It wasn't so much because he was ashamed; he wasn't. It was just that he felt naked now that he wasn't wearing a costume. He thought about putting on a jester's cap and bells, just for old times' sake, but decided against it. No matter what costume he put on, it would make no difference. The *Daily Dynamite* had taken care of that.

There was a light knock at the door. His mother poked her head in.

"Sam, did you read the newspaper today?"

"No, Mom."

"Really? Because there's a story about you in it. You wouldn't believe it!"

"Yes, Mom, I know. It's on the last page."

"Of course it's on the last page. It wouldn't make sense on the front page."

"What do you mean?"

"Well, you can't read it out of order. Didn't you read the articles in the front? Have you not read the editorial?"

"No . . . I didn't read any of the articles. I already know what they say."

"How can you know what they say if you didn't read them?"

"I just know."

Marianne Marblecook, previously Ann-Marie Acker-bloom, snorted. "Hmph! And they call me crazy!" She tossed a copy of the newspaper onto Sam's desk. "Read the editorial," she said. "Oh, and there's a crowd outside who all want to speak to you."

"A crowd? What kind of crowd?" Sam said, bolting to his feet, alarmed.

"Noisy. Angry. The first ones got here about an hour ago, and it's just been growing and growing since then."

"Why didn't you say something earlier?"

"I wanted to give them all appointments, but my book seems to have turned into a box filled with empty brown wrappers that smell like chocolate."

Sam groaned. It felt like he was reliving his nightmare—an angry mob ready to rip him apart and tear down everything he had built. In another era they would have been waving pitchforks and torches. These days they waved their lawyers' phone numbers. Sam covered his face with his hands. He wished he could escape in his Invisiblimp, but somehow the balls had disabled it. Those balls really did have a bad attitude. There wasn't anything he could do but try to reason with these people. Maybe if he apologized, they wouldn't kill him. He took a deep breath and let it out in a long sigh, like a deflating balloon.

"Let them in."

"Let the first one in?"

"No, let them all in. I might as well get this over with."

Sam girded himself, grabbing the fire extinguisher for good measure. The door opened and a swarm of people

entered, yelling and waving copies of the *Daily Dynamite* as Sam stood up behind his desk.

"Please! Please stop shouting! I can't understand you if you all bellow at once. Now, I'm sorry if you are offended by my secrecy, but I stand behind my school and—"

"How dare you!" a woman shouted, the wattle beneath her neck jiggling furiously. "How dare you create such a wonderful, creative learning experience and not make it available to all students?"

"What . . . what was that?" Sam wasn't sure he'd heard correctly. It almost sounded like she had given him a compliment.

"My daughter is a straight-A student at Horsemouth Middle School. All of her teachers love her. That doesn't mean she doesn't come home every night, crying her eyes out about how bored she is and how she wishes there were some way she could enjoy learning instead of hating it. Why can't she come to this school? Why are you leaving her out?"

"I'm sorry, ma'am, but everybody got a flyer over the summer. Perhaps you were out of town."

"Oh, I got the flyer, all right, but it didn't say the school was going to be *amazing.*"

"I'll try to remember to mention that in any subsequent advertising," Sam promised, satisfying the woman, who moved back to make room for the next person.

"You big idiot!" blustered the mayor of Horsemouth, pushing his way to the front. "A school like this could put our town on the map! We won't have to live in Bravington's shadow anymore! How can you hide something like this? Take *that,* Bravington!" he spat.

"I'm a teacher," a young woman said. "I would love to work at an exciting, cutting-edge place like this. We teachers are tired of the boring old methods too. Now, as far as my credentials are concerned, I'm not technically mentally disturbed, but many people consider me to be decidedly odd."

One after another everyone pleaded his or her case, that all children should have access to the school, that it was the most exciting thing to have ever come to Horsemouth, and that they would even be willing to donate money if it would help the school accommodate a larger student body. Sam couldn't believe it. The people in the mob were all shouting ideas and suggestions, not criticisms and curses. Two things became instantly clear: they all liked the school, and in some way they all wanted to be a part of it. Sam buzzed his mother on the intercom.

"Mom! I mean, Mrs. Marblecook! Do you have a pad of paper out there?"

"You know very well I have a thousand," the voice said over the speaker.

"Well, bring one in here! We're signing people up!"

By the end of the day, the crowd had finally thinned out. Sam had twenty pages of names, addresses, and telephone numbers. There were 822 signatures of people interested in enrolling their children at Kaboom Academy the following year, as well as the names of people who had special skills—contractors, architects, artists, and educators—who wanted to join him in his enterprise. The most surprising name on the list was that of Mr. Leonard Gravestone, the principal at Horsemouth Middle School.

"I'm bored too," Leonard explained after signing his name. "I know nobody's happy at Horsemouth Middle School, not the students, not the teachers, not me. But you see, Mr. Ackerbloom, I never wanted to be an educator."

"No? It's a noble profession. . . ."

"I'm sure it is, but I don't have the feel for it. I'm not good at it. The truth is I've been unhappy for a long time. I always pictured myself in a much more exciting career, but somewhere along the way my plans got derailed and I ended up a principal."

"May I ask what it was you wanted to be?" Sam asked.

"A prison guard."

"Ah. That explains a lot," Sam said.

"I hope you will consider taking over Horsemouth Middle," Leonard continued. "It can become a charter school for more autonomy. Or perhaps you can use the campus for your high school. I'm not sure what the legalities are, but we can bring it up with the Horsemouth School Board and the superintendent. I'm sure everyone can come to some sort of agreement. Especially since if things don't change, they won't have a student body. No student body, no school, right?"

"Right," Sam agreed. After a few more pleasant exchanges, Leonard handed Sam his card and left. As Sam quickly scanned the list of names and occupations on his list, what he discovered was that the unremarkable town of Horsemouth was in fact remarkably filled with visionaries like himself, imaginative people with unusual ideas. They had kept their thoughts to themselves, though, fearful that they would be laughed at or, worse, ostracized. All it took was one person to encourage them to come forward, throw off the mantle of conformity, and bare their true selves to the world.

"Ahem."

Sam looked up. It was Winston Leroux, otherwise known as the Great Gumballini. "I'd like a real job at the school, if possible," Winston said. "I'm not doing very well as a musician . . . *magician*."

"All right, what are you good at?" Sam said. He felt he owed Winston something; after all, he'd included the poor man in his deception and had left him exposed to the wrath of the journalism students.

"Well, I'm actually a very talented magician . . . *musician*," Winston said eagerly. "Just listen as I play my foot . . . *flute*." Winston pulled the instrument from his coat and immediately launched into a beautiful and complex classical piece. Sam was impressed by the purity of his tone and the emotion that infused every phrase and each note.

"You're amazing," Sam said once Winston had finished. "Why didn't you work as a musician?"

"My mother always wanted a magician in the family," Winston said sadly. "My feather—*father*—was a magician, and so was his father before him. I much prefer music, though. You don't have to leak as much . . . *speak* as much."

"I'm sure I can find something for you," Sam assured him. "But I really have a lot to think about right now."

Winston gave Sam a little bow, then turned to leave, passing the group of journalism students who had just entered.

"Oh, hi!" Sam said, surprised. "I didn't expect to see you here."

"Are you mad at us?" Jory asked, pointing at the *Daily Dynamite* sitting on Sam's desk.

"Mad? Mad? Of course not! You guys did what you had to do and did it really well. I'm not mad, I'm proud. I mean, you put out a newspaper pretty much on your own! You uncovered a huge scandal! You got people in this town talking . . . and strangely enough, acting. I would never have thought it possible!"

"Yes, we heard it all from the reception area," Edie said. "It sounded as if more people liked the school than cared about its shady beginnings."

"Which is kind of weird, since people from Horsemouth are usually quick to criticize," Ruben pointed out.

"I wonder how public opinion could have been manipulated like that," Victoria said slyly. "It's almost like somebody planned it that way."

Sam looked from one grinning face to another. Then it dawned on him what they had done. "That's why you put the article on the back page!" He turned to Jory. "I thought you were trying to bury it."

"Actually, the placement of the story was Edie's idea," Jory admitted.

"Simple psychology," Edie explained. "I knew that once people read Jory's fantastic editorial and the other articles first, they would find out how great the school was and how lucky the students were to be here. More importantly, they would find out that the students were handpicked. That information would arouse emotions in them that were stronger than mistrust and suspicion: jealousy and desire. I've seen it happen over and over again. Once people decide they want something, they're a lot more forgiving about its flaws."

"Yes, they were very forgiving," Sam agreed. "They were actually supportive . . . thankful, even. I really didn't expect that."

"I did."

"You did?"

Edie sighed. "You really need to have more faith in people, Sam. Once you dig down deep enough, most people are pretty decent. They're just waiting for an opportunity to show it . . . like us, for instance. We came here to tell you that we forgive you for spying on us and that we really do like the school. We actually absolutely love it. It's the best thing that's ever happened to us. We just wish you were back in the classroom."

Victoria stepped forward. "Yeah, we miss our friend Sam and his outlandish costumes and tortured accents."

"Well, that Sam doesn't exist anymore, I'm afraid. There is only me. But once you get to know me, I'm not so bad. And you know," Sam said, rising from his seat, "you don't have a journalism teacher anymore. Mr. Mister really likes it in the gardening shed. He wants to be the groundskeeper. Says it will keep him from having to take out his earplugs. Which means I could come back into the classroom as the journalism teacher."

"But aren't you going to be busy expanding the school?" Jory pointed at the yellow pad filled with contact information and notes.

"Yes . . . well, maybe. I don't want the school to get too unwieldy. But no matter what I decide to do about expansion, I still want to know what students are really thinking. Since I can't be a kid anymore, you guys will have to be my eyes and ears. I want to be in constant contact with you. And I didn't tell you this before, but those letters my dad sent me while he was in prison? They were filled with designs for new and even more spectacular inventions. I could use some youthful input on their development."

"Youthful input? You mean guinea pigs," Victoria said.

"It sounds so sinister when you put it that way," Sam chided. Victoria raised her eyebrows, crossing her arms expectantly. "Okay, fine. Guinea pigs," Sam admitted with a shrug.

"You know, it's not so bad being a guinea pig," Margo piped up. "I've met a few kids who picked that for their detention. Apparently guinea pigs have a wicked sense of humor. You just don't realize it because they're so quiet. But when nobody's looking, they're cutting up constantly."

As the students digested this surprising information, Jory turned back to Sam. "You were saying?" he prompted.

"Oh, right," Sam said. "Anyway, I'd just be your journalism teacher in name, because I really don't know any more about journalism than you do. But obviously, you know a lot—enough to put out an incisive, provocative, and only slightly biased newspaper."

"Speaking of which, we have to do it again," Jory said. "It's time to start working on our next issue."

The teens left Sam's office, waving to Mrs. Marblecook as they headed down the hallway. Already their minds swirled with ideas for new newspaper articles. Victoria was thinking about the refrigerator-shaped package with the words INFINITY BOX stamped on the side that had arrived that morning for the math teacher. Ruben wondered what to make of the sheet he'd seen tacked to Coach Freeman's bulletin board that said "Rules for Human Ping-Pong." Aliya and Taliya had noticed that a desk moved into the science classroom had a card on it stating, "Reserved for Albert Einstein." Margo was certain something interesting was bound to happen at the school dance next weekend; after all, the theme of the dance was "Intelligent Monkeys." Jory's sights were set on the bell tower; he was sure the view and the wind speed would be spectacular from up there. Leo was seriously considering sending in his photographs to compete for various photo contests after classmates remarked on their artistically daring askew composition. And Edie? She had already accomplished her first goal. Her new goal was to find the *second*-most shocking, jaw-dropping story of the year. But what would it be?

EPILOGUE

JORY'S EDITORIAL

PHOTO BY MARIANNE MARBLECOOK

Welcome to the very first issue of the *Daily Dynamite*. We hope that as you read about our school, you will discover what we on the *Dynamite* staff have: that Kaboom Academy is not a school but a portal. Once you step through that gate onto school grounds, you don't know what you will find: peculiar people, inventions that boggle the mind, ideas that confound all reason. Conceived as a place for creative and imaginative

exploration, the school has become more than that. It has become a community.

Back in September, when we first arrived at Kaboom Academy, many of us felt isolated. We felt uncomfortable, like we didn't fit in anywhere. But after only two months, we have learned to reach out to one another, even when we couldn't stand each other! We have learned to tolerate and appreciate our differences. We have discovered that a solution to a problem doesn't always come from where you would expect. We have become friends. We have found ourselves. We have even developed school spirit. Go, Firecrackers!

How did Kaboom Academy accomplish this? It's hard to say, except that as an experimental school, it keeps an open mind about everything. The academy's philosophy reflects that of the man who created it, a man who loves puzzles, games, inventions, and having fun. You will learn more about him on the back page. As you read his story, consider the articles before it, and how every day is extraordinary at Kaboom Academy. There is no other school on the planet that can match it, and here is the proof: so far this year every student has had perfect attendance. Nobody wants to miss a moment.

Read about our adventures and enjoy!

Go, Firecrackers!

Jory Bellard
Editor in Chief

Q: We've heard you always wear earplugs in your ears and that they make it hard for you to hear. Are you wearing them now?

A: *What a strange question! I'm not wearing an entire cow, just a pair of leather shoes.*

Q: Are you bothered by loud sounds?

A: *Isn't everybody bothered by proud hounds? I mean, what does a hound have so much to be proud about? Whenever I see a dog strutting around putting on airs, it really ticks me off. Except Labrador retrievers. I think they might actually be better than us.*

Q: Have you always wanted to teach?

A: *I would love to go to the beach, but there isn't one around for miles.*

Q: Do you have any hobbies?

A: *No, I don't own any hoggies, piggies, donkeys, duckies, or any other livestock. And I'd appreciate it if you stopped using baby talk. I'm a grown man.*

Q: Do you consider yourself a newsman?

A: *That question is really inappropriate! Of course I'm not a nude man! You can see very well I'm fully clothed!*

Q: How do you feel about your odd name?

A: I would never feel a cod's brain. First of all, I'm not sure I could identify it among all the other cod parts. What does it look like? I have no idea. Secondly, I have better things to do with my time.

Q: How did you spend your summer?

A: I don't think spending makes you dumber, though I've seen people buy some pretty dumb-looking outfits.

Q: Are you married?

A: No, I'm not very merry, I have to admit. I'm more the serious type.

Q: Do you have any advice for the Kaboom Academy students?

A: No, all my rice I keep for myself. I certainly wouldn't use it for stewed ants. I'm not much for eating insects. I prefer hamburgers.

Q: Thank you for your time.

A: I haven't given you my tie, and you can't have it.

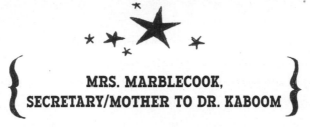

{ MRS. MARBLECOOK, SECRETARY/MOTHER TO DR. KABOOM }

Q: How did you meet your husband, George Ackerbloom, Dr. Kaboom's father?

A: I met George at a toy shop. We were both about twenty-five. He was bringing samples of his gadgets and toys around to different stores, holding demonstrations to get people interested. He was so funny and lively, with his big barbershop mustache and his beautiful blue eyes. His toys were frankly amazing, so I bought one of each, fifteen items altogether. That got his attention. He asked me how many kids I had and I told him I didn't have any kids, I'd never been married, and the toys were for me. He later said to me he knew right then that we were made for each other.

Q: What was it like being married to an inventor of novelty toys and gadgets?

A: It was great fun, but I always had to be prepared for a surprise. Once I turned on the television and it showed the news from 1944. That was strange. Another time I lay down in my water bed and discovered it had been turned into a Jell-O bed. It was actually quite comfortable! And delicious!

Q: We understand that you are a hoarder, someone who accumulates more things than is reasonable. Is that true?

A: Yes, I collect office supplies. Fun fact: I believe I've accumulated enough to supply the Pentagon, which is the largest office building in the United States.

Q: When did you realize you were a hoarder?
A: When I collected my sixty-third three-hole puncher. Somehow owning sixty-two three-hole punchers seemed reasonable, but when I got the sixty-third I knew I had a problem.

Q: What is it like to be a hoarder?
A. I'm not proud of my hoarding. The worst part is trying to find space to keep all my stuff. My house and backyard are crammed with office supplies, getting dustier by the minute. No housekeeper will ever agree to work for me.

Q: Do you have any advice for fellow hoarders who would like to kick the habit?
A: Yes, seek help before you lose all your friends. I mean literally lose them in your junk. It happened to me; it can happen to you too. With help from a psychologist and a bulldozer, I was able to get my habit under control, though I sometimes fall back into old habits. My heart still races when I see a box of paper clips.

Q: What is your favorite thing to do when you're not at work?
A: Arrange my staplers. I have 23,455 staplers of all sizes and colors, so it's quite a project.

Q: How did you spend your summer vacation?
A: Arranging my staplers.

Q: Have you ever invented anything?
A: Not yet, but I'm working on a key ring for hoarders. People like me need a key ring that's so big we can't miss it. I tried using

a shoe, but of course I have hundreds of shoes, so I could never remember which one I'd used. I tried putting it on a little dog so I could just call the dog and get the key, but it was hard keeping the dog in my purse. I tried attaching it to a piece of rotting meat so I could just smell where it was, but you can imagine why that didn't work.

Q: What is it like living in a psychiatric hospital?
A: You get to meet the most interesting people. My neighbor on one side once refused to speak and would only communicate by whistling through a straw he'd stuck in his nostril. The woman who lived across the hall from me insisted she was a chicken. I got fresh eggs from her every morning, so I wasn't about to tell her otherwise.

Q: Do you ever feel like collecting something other than office supplies?
A: No, I'm trying to live more simply. From now on I just want to collect friends.

MR. PARKER, JANITOR/FACILITY MANAGER

Q: You know everything about this facility. Are there any secrets?
A: Yes.

Q: What are they?
A: If I told you, they wouldn't be secrets anymore.

Q: What did you do before you had this job?
A: I worked for the government. That's all I can say.

Q: What's the biggest mess you've had to clean up?
A: Before the school opened, there had been talk about it being a self-sustaining enterprise; that is, growing the food that the kids would eat in the cafeteria right here on campus, on a farm at the back of the facility. Lunch Lady Lois started experimenting with potato-chip trees, but when the time came to harvest the chips it was a disaster. The chips were carried on the breeze. They floated all over the place and landed everywhere. Once they hit the ground, if they were there for more than five seconds we couldn't feed them to the kids. And because the chips were all over the campus, it was impossible to sweep, shovel, or spray them away. I ended up bringing in a drove of pigs to clean it up. Of course, then I had to clean up what the pigs left behind, which was even worse.

Q: Is the construction of the school finished?
A: Because this is an experimental school, the campus is constantly

changing. We'll get rid of the things that don't work and try to add buildings, classrooms, and other elements to the facility that we think will be of use. For instance, right now we have a very nice library that contains resources to supply students with factual information, but we are planning to build a lie-brary to supply them with an equal amount of nonsense.

Q: Do you have any advice for students?
A: Please pick up after yourselves. Kaboom Academy has an aggressive recycling program. Anything left lying around on the ground will be collected and recycled, including sleeping students.

Q: Are you married? Do you have a family?
A: I am not married. I live right here on the Kaboom Academy campus, in the silo that looks like a rocket ship.

Q: Is it a rocket ship?
A: As far as you know, no.

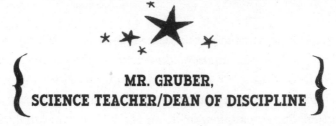

MR. GRUBER,
SCIENCE TEACHER/DEAN OF DISCIPLINE

Q: You teach several different science classes at Kaboom Academy. Which is your favorite?

A: I teach earth science, life science, and biology, but my specialty is theoretical science, which deals with hypothetical speculations rather than practical applications.

Q: That's a difficult concept. Could you explain what theoretical science is in more detail?

A: Think of it as science of the imagination. My job is to theorize about abstract notions, then make conjectural guesses about ideas that are wholly academic.

Q: Could you please simplify your description even further?

A: I think about science stuff.

Q: As the dean of discipline you use hypnotism to relax students serving detention by getting them to focus on lab animals and "become" the animal for several hours. How did you happen upon this method?

A: I call it "hypnotherapy." I had some very disruptive students in my class, and as I tried to think of ways to quiet them down, I noticed the class guinea pigs lying calmly in their cage, eating carrots. At that moment I thought how wonderful it would be if the hooligans could find the same inner peace as the guinea pigs. The hypnotism achieves just that. An extra benefit is that the therapy encourages the students to eat more vegetables, which are sorely lacking in the diets of most middle schoolers.

Q: What about students who focus on nonvegetarian animals, such as the snakes or the frogs? Have their diets also improved?
A: Well, the school's rodent and mosquito populations have been reduced considerably. That's all I'll say about that.

Q: What is it like working with Dr. Kaboom?
A: As you can imagine, it is very gratifying to work with a visionary inventor like Dr. Kaboom; however, he has a habit of turning my theoretical musings into reality, so I have to be careful what I say to him. We were talking about genetic splicing and I told him a joke: What happens when you cross a cat with some wood? You get a catalog. Get it? Cat-a-log? The next thing I knew there were some very disturbing cords of wood with yellow eyes and persnickety attitudes. I hadn't meant for my mild and frankly unfunny joke to be used as a suggestion for an actual science experiment, but there you have it.

Q: Are you saying there are living feline logs somewhere on the Kaboom Academy campus?
A: Yes, but they're hard to find. Like most cats, they won't come when you call them. Many of them climbed into trees and have blended in so that you can no longer tell they're there.

Q: We understand that you have a particular dislike of yo-yos and had them banned from the campus. Are there any other toys that you don't like?

A: I'm not fond of jacks either. I've had more than one jack fly into my ear after being hit by that little pink ball and then ricocheting skyward. People don't talk a lot about jacks-related injuries, but those little things are killers. They're like miniature ninja throwing stars.

Q: Do you have any advice for the students?
A: If you do happen to get detention and must undergo hypnotherapy, consider focusing on the mealworms. Nobody ever chooses the mealworms, and they're beginning to take it personally.